If Tw
Ar
De

The Sandy and David Mysteries:

Mystery at Black Rock Island
The Ghost of Ramshaw Castle
The Loon Lake Murders
Death Island

Other Scholastic titles by this author:

Son of the Hounds
Suddenly a Spy

ROBERT SUTHERLAND

If Two Are Dead

cover by
BERNARD LEDUC

Scholastic Canada Ltd.

Scholastic Canada Ltd.
123 Newkirk Road, Richmond Hill, Ontario, Canada L4C 3G5

Scholastic Inc.
555 Broadway, New York, NY 10012, USA

Ashton Scholastic Pty Limited
PO Box 579, Gosford, NSW 2250, Australia

Scholastic New Zealand Limited
Private Bag 94407, Greenmount, Auckland, New Zealand

Scholastic Publications Ltd.
Villiers House, Clarendon Avenue. Leamington Spa,
Warwickshire CV32 5PR, UK

Canadian Cataloguing in Publication Data

Sutherland, Robert, 1925-
If two are dead

ISBN 0-590-24976-2

I. Title.

PS8587.U798I3 1997   jC813'.54   C96-931971-1
PZ7.S97If 1997

5 4 3 2 1   Printed in Canada   7 8 9/9

For Angus and Sandra, with love.

"Three may keep a secret,
if two of them are dead."
— *Benjamin Franklin*

The telephone rang in an office high above Bay Street. A man in an impeccable grey suit lifted the receiver.

"Yes?"

"We may have a problem."

"What problem?"

"Old man McCrimmon is dead."

"Dead?" A pause. "That was to be expected sooner or later. Who owns the property now?"

"It's taken some scrambling, but I've come up with a name. Some distant relative named Calvin McCrimmon. He's a high school teacher in Woodstock."

"A teacher. In Woodstock." The man in grey looked first at a calendar, then at the map he had pulled from his desk drawer. His eyes travelled west from Toronto along Highway 401. "School reopens in a few days, and Woodstock is a long way from Lost Lake. The probate and paperwork alone could take a year. There's no problem. Not yet."

1

"But there's more to it than that. I guess this McCrimmon guy must be anxious to find out what he inherited. He's sending his son up to look it over. He reserved rooms in the Collinton motel for next Friday night."

"His son? How old?"

"Don't know. He's still in school, but he must be old enough to drive."

"I fail to see your problem." There was a hint of impatience in the voice. "All you have to do is discourage him from going to the lodge. Prevent him, if necessary. You do understand me?"

"Right. I get you." The caller hung up.

The man in grey ran his eye over one of many invoices. The bottom figure was impressively high.

1

"This is it. This is where we spend the night — the closest town to Lost Lake." David squinted to block out the glare from the sun setting below the surrounding hills. "Dad reserved rooms for us in a motel here in Collinton. That will give us the best part of two days to explore our new property."

Sandy looked over at him. "Are you excited?"

"Yes, I guess I am. We've always wanted property on an unspoiled lake. Unfortunately there don't seem to be many of those left. And to be handed one like this! I'd never even heard of great-great-uncle David. Or should there be another 'great' in there?"

She laughed. "It's going to be fun if it's anything like Loon Lake. We had a super time there — in spite of a murder or two."

"Well, there won't be anything like that this time, I hope. But the area should be very much like Loon Lake. Hills and rocks and trees and lots of wildlife. And the lake of course."

They passed the sprawling yards of the Collinton Lumber Mills and slowed as they started down what was apparently the main street.

"Watch for a motel now," said David. "It's supposed to be right in town. 'You can't miss it,' they told Dad."

"There's one! The Rest Easy."

"That's it. And they were right. We couldn't miss it — not with a sign like that." The name of the motel flashed continuously in neon lights. David pulled into a driveway that led to an office door, sheltered under an extended roof. There was another smaller sign here, over the door: *Rest Easy Motel. Bruce and Julia Beakham, Props.* Beyond the office was the line of rooms, each with a draped window from which an air conditioner jutted. It looked clean and recently repainted.

"Looks all right," David said. "You never know what to expect, especially if there's only one motel to choose from." He hesitated before opening his door. "Are you hungry yet, Sandy?"

She shook her head. "Not particularly."

"Neither am I. Let's check in, then go a bit farther along the north road before coming back for supper. Maybe we'll go as far as the forest road that's marked on the map — just to save time looking for it in the morning. I'm anxious to get to Lost Lake as early as we can tomorrow."

"So am I." As Sandy opened her car door the humid air wrapped around her. "Wouldn't I like to be able to jump into a cool lake right now," she said to David over the roof of the car.

"I guess you'll have to make do with just a shower until tomorrow. Whew, I didn't realize it was so hot. I'm happy to see those air conditioners. Let's find out which rooms are ours."

A bell rang somewhere in the interior as he pushed open the door to the office, and a moment later a man appeared through an inner door. He had a nose like the prow of a ship, its sharpness accentuated by a receding forehead and chin. With a name like Beakham and a nose like that, thought David, I can guess what they call him behind his back. He stifled a grin.

"Yes?" The man smiled a toothy smile. "Can I help you?"

"I hope so. You should have two rooms reserved for us. Name of McCrimmon."

"Indeed I have." The man ruffled through a pile of cards and withdrew two. "You will be David McCrimmon? I'm Bruce Beakham. Welcome to Collinton. That will be for just the one night?"

"Yes. We're on our way to Lost Lake, but it's kind of late to do that tonight. We've never been here

5

before, and we don't want to have to find it in the dark. Are you familiar with it?"

"Lost Lake?" Mr. Beakham frowned and shook his head. "The name sounds familiar, but I don't recall . . . But of course, there are lots of lakes in the general area. You can find it in the daylight all right, can you?"

"Yes, we have a good map. Apparently there's what's called a summer track running off a forest road."

"That's good. Now, if you will sign here, David. And —" he turned to the other card, then to Sandy "— you will be Sandra MacLeod?"

"Actually," she said, "it's Alexandra. But everyone calls me Sandy."

"Right. Sandy. You're from Woodstock too?"

"No, Scotland."

"Scotland! Well, well, a long-distance visitor. I supppose I should have guessed that from your accent, and that curly red hair. If you will sign here? And here are your keys. Rooms eleven and twelve, just along there." He pointed. "Now, is there anything I can do for you? You'll be wanting a meal before long, I expect. The Pagoda's good. It's just down the next block."

"Thanks, we'll remember that. We're going to take a drive first to locate the forest road that's marked on the map. Then we'll be back. We go straight through town, do we?"

"For the north road? That's right." He looked out the window to where the McCrimmon's Jeep Cherokee stood in the driveway, a red canoe lashed to the roof rack. "I see you have a four-wheel drive. That's good. You may need it if you're going to — what is it? — Lost Lake."

"That's what we thought." David picked up the keys. "Thanks, Mr. Beakham."

They stopped before room number eleven. David gave Sandy her key, then paused when he noticed her expression. "What's up? You look puzzled."

"Oh. Are my thoughts that easy to read? I was just wondering. First Mr. Beakham said he wasn't familiar with Lost Lake. Then he said it's a good thing we have a four-wheel drive if we're going there. That struck me as odd. How did he know?"

David shrugged. "As he said, there are lots of lakes in the area. They're probably all alike — not very accessible. Now, what do you think? Do you want to have a shower before we go? I didn't expect it to be so hot."

"No, I'll leave that till later. It's cool in the car. Just give me ten minutes."

A few moments later they headed out of the driveway and onto the street. A pick-up truck pulled away from the curb behind them, and kept pace with them as they drove out of town and along the north road.

2

The hills were higher north of Collinton. The road wound up above deep ravines or cut through towering outcrops of granite. Even so, the grades were long, the hills steep and the corners sharp. Frequent signs warned of the probability of deer and moose crossing the road.

David drove just under the posted limit, letting the occasional car pass. This was the kind of country he loved, with its seas of evergreens, its hardwoods beginning to glow with autumn colours, its sparkling lakes and tumbling streams, and now and then a glimpse of a white-tailed deer.

He glanced across at Sandy. She had the map partly folded on her lap, but she was ignoring it, watching the passing scenery.

"Look!" she said, pointing. "Down there by that

lake. A bull moose. Look at those antlers!"

"Let's just hope he keeps them," David said. "That rack would make quite a trophy on some hunter's wall."

"And that's allowed here?" Sandy asked. "What a shame. Who could hunt such magnificent animals?"

"There are hunting seasons for deer, moose, and bear," he said. "Not very long, any of them. They're supposed to keep the numbers down to manageable proportions. And to give hunters something to shoot at, of course. I could never do that myself."

She shook her head. "Me neither. You're so lucky to have the sort of wildlife you do here. I suppose there are game wardens to keep the hunting regulated at least."

David didn't answer right away. There was a truck behind them. A pick-up. He had noticed it earlier, and had expected it to pass. But it didn't. Apparently the driver was in no more of a hurry than he was.

"There are people who hunt out of season, of course . . ." The truck was speeding up, gaining on the Jeep. "I don't think it's any great problem around here, though . . ." The truck was right behind them now. David eased off on the accelerator and edged over near the shoulder. There was a straight stretch ahead, and no traffic in sight. A good place for the truck to pass.

"Look!" Sandy was pointing again. "A big bird. A heron —"

But David was watching his rear-view mirror. "Come on," he muttered. "Pass if you're going to."

Apparently he *was* going to. The truck pulled out, abruptly gunning ahead. For a moment it was beside the Jeep, its engine roaring. David had a brief glimpse of the driver hunched over the wheel, his face shadowed beneath a baseball cap. He was close. Too close. David edged farther over until the right wheels were on the narrow shoulder. "Watch it," he hissed. A shallow grade right beside the road led to a steep drop-off into a deep ravine.

The other driver suddenly seemed to realize that he was too close. The truck veered away. David felt momentary relief, relief that died an abrupt death. With the sudden swerve the other driver seemed to lose control. The truck came back, right into their path, cutting them off. The box over its back wheels struck the front fender of the Jeep, jarring the steering wheel in David's hands. He clutched it, trying to counter the thrust of truck, but it was no use. They were going off the road. There was only one thing to save them from rolling the Jeep.

He yanked the wheel to the right. If they were going, they were going down straight, nose first. It was their only chance. He hoped he was in time.

The front wheel hit the edge, locked. The Jeep shuddered, threatened to roll, then righted. They were hurtling down the slope that gradually dropped away from the road. And then, David realized in a flash of panic, the slope sheered off into a deep ravine only a few car lengths away. Boulders like giant teeth awaited them far below. Nothing but a tree, clinging to the lip of the ravine, stood between them and empty space.

He slammed the brakes to the floor. They grabbed. But still the Jeep was moving, sliding on locked wheels. He hauled back on the steering wheel, white-knuckled, as if he could drag the Jeep to a halt. The left front wheel hit something, jarring the steering wheel in his hands. Brush dragged across their underbelly, slowing them. But still they were moving, sliding relentlessly, and there was nothing but that tree to stop them. Some day it would be a stout cedar. But that was years in the future. Right now, standing alone between them and death, it seemed little more than a sapling.

The slide towards the cedar must have been a matter of seconds, but to David and Sandy it was a lifetime, a lifetime in slow motion. They should release their seat belts and bail out. They both knew that. But it was as if shock held them powerless as the Jeep slid inexorably forward. And the single tree stood waiting for them.

They hit it. It bent over, far out over the gorge. The Jeep rode onto it. Something gave. But it wasn't the tree.

The wheels! David thought wildly. They're over the edge! He was aware of the hood springing up, of a sudden eruption of steam. But that didn't matter. They were no longer moving. The tree had saved them.

For what seemed an eternity neither he nor Sandy moved. They sat paralysed, scarcely daring to breathe.

Sandy spoke first. "Thank God," she whispered. "Thank God for that tree."

David tried to answer, but he had no voice. He fumbled for the door handle, but his hands were trembling. He clamped them between his knees. At last his voice came back.

"We'll have to go carefully," he said. "I don't know how secure we are. We better not make any sudden movements." He released his seat belt and reached again for the door handle. Sandy did the same.

"Okay," he said. "We'll both go at the same time. Be quick, just in case."

She nodded. They opened their doors simultaneously and rolled out onto the ground. The Jeep quivered, but stayed.

It had stopped at the brink. Its front end rested on the bowed trunk of the tree, overhanging the gorge. The wheel on the driver's side was on the very edge of the ravine, the rim bent, the tire flat.

David shuddered. He didn't want to move. He

wanted to sit there on the hillside while his nerves calmed and his guts settled down. He looked through the opened doorways to check on Sandy but saw no sign of her. Another flush of panic. "Sandy!"

"Just a minute."

He slumped in relief. She was all right. He stood on shaky legs and went around the Jeep. She was sitting there, much as he had been, her eyes large in a white face.

"My knees gave out," she said. "You'd think I was scared silly, wouldn't you. And you'd be absolutely right." She reached out a hand to him.

He pulled her up and hugged her.

"Now," said David, after a moment, "we'd better climb back up to the road and flag down a car. We'll have to notify the police. And Dad. He's going to have a fit. And the insurance company."

"Where on earth is the driver of that truck? He must have seen what happened."

"You'd think so. But maybe he was too busy trying to regain control to notice what happened to us. We can't count on him anyway."

It was a scramble to reach the road. When they made the top the sweat was running into their eyes. The sun had vanished behind the western hills but the humid air still lingered.

They were standing on the shoulder of the road, still catching their breath, when a car approached from the north. David stepped forward, waving his arms.

The car pulled over. The driver rolled his window down. "What's up? Are you in trouble?"

"Yes, we are." David was surprised that his voice was still unsteady. "Our car is down there." He pointed down toward the ravine. "We were run off the road —"

"Down *there?*" The driver whistled. "Obviously you didn't go all the way over or you wouldn't be here. Are you all right? Is anyone hurt?" He looked across the road at Sandy. "Is the girl okay?"

"Yes, we're both fine. But we'll have to call the police."

"Let me take a look." The driver pushed open his door. He was a big man, florid, rumpled, and hearty. "I'm Walter Stewart, of the *Collinton Echo*. Also of radio station CKOW. So you'll pardon me if I ask some nosy questions."

David followed the driver across the road and pointed down at the Cherokee, with its front end resting on the tree and a wisp of steam rising from the radiator. The red canoe was, miraculously, still fastened to the roof.

Walter Stewart whistled again. "That," he said, "was close. There's no one else down there, is there? You're sure you're not hurt? I think we should call the ambulance and have you both checked over."

"No, no," said David. "We're both fine. A little

shaken up maybe, but okay otherwise."

Stewart turned to Sandy. "Is that correct?" She nodded. "All right, if you're sure . . . Now you said you were *run* off the road?"

David nodded. "A pick-up was passing and he cut in too close in front of us. His back end hit our fender and there was nothing I could do but try to go down there head first instead of sideways. I guess the driver didn't know what happened. Anyway he didn't stop. Did you pass a black pick-up back there?"

"Yes, I believe I did, though I couldn't say for sure. First, though, we'd better call the police. And a tow truck. I'll contact my office and get things going. Then you two had better wait in my car until help arrives." He grinned. "While you're waiting you can tell me all about yourselves. I'm a newsman, remember."

*　　*　　*

"This is Sandy MacLeod," David began when they were seated in the back of Walter Stewart's Buick. "She's visiting from Scotland. I'm David McCrimmon. We're on our way to Lost Lake —"

"Wait a minute. McCrimmon. Lost Lake. You must be related to the owner." Stewart was seated crosswise on the front seat, his back against the door. "Don't tell me he's finally going to do something with that old lodge?"

"Well, actually, he's dead — the original owner,

I mean. He was my dad's great-uncle. He's been living in Australia for years, and he left the property to us in his will. I guess we're his only relatives in Canada. Dad couldn't come up here. He's a teacher, and school opens next week. So I'm here to look it over and take pictures back to my parents so we can make plans for next year. We really know very little about the property. We never even knew it existed until this week."

"I might be able to help you out there. Early in the century lumber barons began to build railways into the wilderness to bring out the lumber. There were no roads, of course. Then some people got the idea of building lodges beside the railways to bring in hunters and fishermen from the cities, and from the States."

David nodded. "I've heard about that. Weren't some built in Algonquin Park?"

"That's right. And your — great-uncle, is it? — uncle's lodge sits beside one of the spur lines north of here, on the shore of Lost Lake."

"But that must have been ages ago. Those lodges all disappeared years back, didn't they?"

"Most did. The railways declined, of course, as roads were built. The leases of those in Algonquin were never renewed, as I understand it, and the park reverted to a more natural state. There was never any road in to Lost Lake, and I guess the decline in business persuaded your uncle that it wouldn't be worthwhile to put one in. I suppose that's why he abandoned the lodge. As far as I know, he sold off the fixtures and furniture as best he could, and just walked away and left it."

"So, is the lodge still standing?"

"Who knows? But in any case it will have deteriorated badly over the years. It's the lake that's worth something. I wouldn't be surprised if it's pollution free — and probably teeming with fish. No one ever goes in there. I'll bet it's thirty kilometres back in the bush, and as I said there never was a road in to it."

"But there *is* a road. Well, maybe not a road exactly. But we have one of those detailed topographical maps, and it shows a forest road off this one —" Mr. Stewart nodded "— and then what's labelled Lost Road. It's described as a summer track."

"Is that right? I wasn't aware of that. But I can guess what's happened. Someone *has* been fishing in there, without bothering to ask anyone's permission. And you can't blame a person for that. No one knew where the owner had gone to. Likely someone's been going in often enough to make your 'summer track.'"

David nodded. "Well, whoever it was, he's welcome to it. Dad likes to fish, but he's not one to keep good fishing to himself if there's plenty of it."

"That's the spirit. He'll be a good neighbour. It's

too bad he couldn't make it up here himself. How about you? You won't be going to Lost Lake today, obviously. Can you wait around till we get your car fixed?"

David shrugged his shoulders. "It doesn't look like it. We only have a couple of days. Then I'm due back at school and Sandy flies back to Scotland."

"That's too bad. But we'll look forward to meeting you all next year — Oh, good. Here come the police."

The OPP cruiser pulled up across the road and two officers got out. They took a quick look over the edge at the Cherokee, then turned. One of them nodded to Stewart, then addressed David.

"You're the driver? What happened?"

"We were forced off the road when a pick-up cut us off."

"Was anyone injured? No? You're sure? All right. You're very lucky. Can I see your driver's licence and owner's permit, please?"

While one constable looked at David's documents, the other was examining the road for tire marks.

"You are David McCrimmon?" the first constable continued. "And the car belongs to Calvin McCrimmon. Your father? Right. I'm Constable Jeff Wilks." He offered his hand to David. His grip was firm. "This young lady?"

"I'm Sandy MacLeod."

"You were a passenger? And you're sure you're not injured? We can get you to a doctor and have you checked over. It's always best to be doubly sure, after something like this."

Sandy pondered. If they went to a doctor they could well end up on their way back to Woodstock without ever laying eyes on Lost Lake. Time was already short enough. "Thank you," she said, "but I'm fine, really. Just a bit shaken up."

The officer shrugged. "If you're sure." He turned to the other officer, who had straightened up again. "This is Auxiliary Constable Ketchawa. What do you think, Dan?"

Dan Ketchawa turned his dark eyes their way. He was wearing the full uniform of an OPP constable, except that he was unarmed. "I would say the tire marks bear out their story. Looks like they were forced off the road."

Constable Wilks nodded. "All right. David, what can you tell us about the truck?"

David closed his eyes in an effort to visualize the pick-up in his rear-view mirror. He recalled the oval logo. "It was a Ford. With horizontal bars in the grill. And it was black. That's about all I can tell you."

"What about the driver?"

David shook his head. "It happened so fast . . . All I can say is that he was wearing a baseball cap."

Constable Wilks laughed. "Like ninety percent

of the men around here. Did the truck actually make contact with you?"

"Yes. It hit my left front fender. It seemed like he lost control when he pulled out to pass. He came too close, and hitting us didn't help any."

"But he didn't stop." Dan Ketchawa was rubbing his nose thoughtfully. "That makes it hit-and-run. And almost vehicular homicide. He must have seen what happened to you. Why didn't he stop when he regained control?"

"I can guess the answer to that," said Constable Wilks. "The truck was stolen."

"Stolen?" Stewart stepped closer. "Why do you say that, Jeff?"

"*Because* he didn't stop. And because a black Ford pick-up was reported stolen this morning. My guess is it's the same one. Have you called for a tow truck yet?"

"Yes. Bill Blake should be here any minute."

"I'm going down to take a look at the car," Dan Ketchawa said. "Would you care to come, David, and tell me again what happened?"

"Sure." David was glad of something to do.

Dan Ketchawa turned to Sandy. "Would you like to wait for us in the cruiser?"

"No, I'll come down with you if that's all right."

David retold how the accident had occurred, while Sandy added her observations and the constable walked around the Jeep, whistling tunelessly between his teeth as he examined the damage.

"The impact on the front fender of your Cherokee seems to support your story," he said. "I'll just add that to Constable Wilks's report, and you'll have to sign it." Then, as he noted David's grim expression, he added, "It wasn't your fault, from what we can tell. If your father gives you a hard time, tell him to get in touch with me. If you hadn't thought to steer straight down the slope, his Jeep might be a total wreck, and he quite possibly would have lost his son."

David nodded. Suddenly his hands started to shake again. He thrust them into his pockets.

"There's not as much damage as you might expect," the officer continued. "Good thing for you this Cherokee stands so high off the ground, or it would have been much more serious. Bill Blake will be able to fix you up — at least to get you running so you can drive home. Where is that, by the way?"

"Woodstock. Near London."

"I know the area. Sorry your trip has been ruined. All right, we can go back up now, and you can sign the report."

When they reached the top they found that the tow truck had arrived. It was a big, powerful vehicle, strong enough to tow the gigantic lumber trucks that rumbled along the forest roads. It should have no trouble hauling the Cherokee out of the ravine, David thought, though getting the hook attached without sending the Jeep plunging farther down could be tricky.

This proved to be the case. They watched as the operator, a sandy-haired man wearing a Montreal Canadiens baseball cap, positioned the hook on the rear axle, scrambled back up the slope, then eased the damaged vehicle up the hillside and onto the road. He lowered the hoist to set the Jeep's wheels down, and hopped out of the cab.

"Who's the owner?"

"I am." David stepped forward. "At least, I'm the driver. My dad owns it. I'm David McCrimmon."

"How are you, David. I'm Bill Blake." He extended a big hand. "At first glance it looks as if you got off light. The damage doesn't appear to be all that bad."

"Can you fix it?"

"Oh sure. But if you're wondering how soon, you'll have to wait till I get it into the shop and take a good look underneath. I can do that right away, if you want. Would you like to come back with me?"

"Yes, that would be best." David turned to Sandy. "We can drop you off at the motel if you want, and I'll join you as soon as I know the worst."

"No, I want to come with you . . ."

"What's this?" Stewart's booming voice broke in on them. "You're staying in a motel, are you?"

"Yes, the Rest Easy."

"Then you can be my guests for supper. At the Pagoda, just down the road from the motel. Shall we say eight o'clock?"

"That's very kind of you. But you really don't need to —"

"I won't take no to an offer of our Collinton hospitality, now. I'll see you both later. And good luck at the garage."

*   *   *

Less than an hour later Bill Blake completed his examination of the Cherokee.

"Good news, David. There's minimal damage underneath — just a dented oil pan, but that doesn't matter. I can fix everything else up so at least she'll get you home. Of course, she won't look too good. I don't do body work. But she'll run."

David took a deep breath of relief. "Thank goodness. Could you do it tomorrow?"

"Sure. In fact, if I scramble — plus if I've got the parts and you authorize some overtime — I could do most of it tonight. You could get away early in the morning."

"You're kidding! Hear that, Sandy? I'll phone Dad and get his okay. And I guess I'll have to get in touch with the insurance company. Is there a Co-Operators agent in town?"

"Yep. Her number's over by the phone. I expect she could get over here in ten minutes. Knowing her, she'd rather pay me overtime than have to rent

23

you a car or pay an extra night or two's motel bill."

"Thanks a lot, Mr. Blake. We really appreciate it. Sandy, maybe we're going to make it to Lost Lake tomorrow after all."

3

Only a few people were seated at the Pagoda restaurant when Walter Stewart ushered Sandy and David in. The dining room was decorated with Chinese lanterns and paintings. A man hurried over to greet them.

"Ah, Walter," he said. "How are you this evening? A table for three?"

"Yes, please, Sun. This is Sun Ying. David and Sandy." The man grinned and bowed, led them to a table, handed them menus, then bustled off to take an order.

A number of people at other tables nodded or waved to Walter Stewart. He acknowledged them and called the waiter back over.

"What do you recommend, Sun?"

The man spread his hands. "Everything."

"And so you should, but that's not much help. Sandy, it's your choice. I can vouch that the Chinese food here is excellent. And the egg rolls are out of this world."

"Then that's what we'll have." Sandy smiled, then scanned the menu. "How does moo goo guy pan, sweet and sour ribs, and pineapple chicken sound? And egg rolls, of course." Both David and their host nodded. "Fine. That should be plenty, I think."

"Right away, Miss."

"Now, while we're waiting for our food, let me get some facts for my story. How did you feel, David, when you first found out you'd inherited a lodge?" Stewart set a tape recorder on the table and asked David a dozen questions, interrupting now and then to clarify a point, or to adjust the volume. When he had all the facts he needed, he turned the machine off and tucked it into his jacket.

"Hmm," he said. "I'm afraid I've centred you two out as celebrities by interviewing you here. Mind if I introduce you around to some of the locals?" Without waiting for an answer he spun around in his seat to address the whole dining room. "Folks, I have here two visitors, David McCrimmon and Sandy MacLeod. David is from Woodstock, down near London. And Sandy is from Scotland. I'm sorry to say their car was forced off the road earlier today, about ten kilometres north of town. But I'm happy to say that no one was hurt, and Bill Blake is going to fix the car up."

"That's good news anyway."

David glanced up at the familiar voice. Yes, there was Bruce Beakham, the proprietor of the Rest Easy Motel, seated in a side booth. "Your car's in good hands. And if you have to stay another night, we'll make sure your rooms are still available. Right, Julia?"

The woman seated across from him nodded. "Certainly. Just in case you need them."

"That's awfully kind of you," David said. "Everyone has been very good to us."

"The McCrimmons," resumed Stewart, "are the new owners of Lost Lake. I understand they inherited it from the last owner, who recently died in Australia. David and Sandy were going in tomorrow to look over the property. Any of you know anything about Lost Lake you can tell them? You might be more familiar with it than I am."

"It seems to me I've heard of it," said Julia Beakham, wrinkling her forehead and tapping the handle of her fork on the table. "Where is it?"

"No one knows. That's why it's called Lost Lake." A big barrel-chested man laughed at his own joke. He wore wide red suspenders over a plaid shirt. A lumberman's hard hat lay on the table in front of him.

"That's a good one, Bull." The man who spoke

sat by himself, lingering over a cup of coffee which he held in both hands as if to warm either the coffee or his hands. He turned to the Beakhams' table. "That's where the old lodge used to be. The haunted lodge. You remember it, Beak?"

Haunted? David glanced across at Sandy. Her eyes met his, bright with excitement.

"Oh, yes," nodded Beakham. "Perhaps I do remember hearing about it. You remember, Julia? No, I guess not. That was boy stuff. The older boys used to dare us kids to go and spend the night in the lodge. We never did, of course — it must be thirty klicks back in the bush, and we had no way of getting there. Right, George?"

"Yeah." The man with the coffee cup nodded. "But the older boys never dared go in either, for all their talk." He grinned. "I know. I was one of them. No, we believed the stories about ghosts and the evil spirits."

"Ghosts and evil spirits?" David turned to their host. "Have you heard anything like that?"

Stewart shrugged. "Vaguely. A newspaper man hears all sorts of tales. And I suppose some people believe such things. In fact, I recall there was a murder there many years ago, and murdered people come back to haunt the scene of the crime, so they say. Maybe that's what started the rumours about the ghost. It'd be interesting to look it up in our files."

The man with the red suspenders poured a generous helping of ketchup over his fries. "Maybe you kids are lucky you didn't make it to Lost Lake. Like George says, there's ghosts and evil spirits. The Indians won't go near the place, and if *they* won't, I sure won't."

"Come on, Bull," laughed George. "You were never scared of anything in your life."

"I'm not scared," grunted Bull. "Just careful. I don't walk into something I don't understand. When it comes to ghosts, I listen to the Indians. They know all about such things."

"I don't know if that's a compliment or not." No one seemed to have noticed the man who spoke. He swung round, now, on his bar stool, to face the dining room.

"It's Dan What's-his-name," whispered Sandy. "The auxiliary constable."

Dan Ketchawa's black eyes gleamed, reflecting the light over the bar. "We know all about those things, do we Bull?"

"Dan! I didn't see you sitting there." Bull sounded uneasy.

"Hello, Dan." George took a sip of his coffee. "*You* know anything about Lost Lake?"

"Not much." He looked over at Sandy and David. "If it's haunted, as they say, maybe it's just as well you're going home when the car is fixed, instead of to Lost Lake."

"Oh, but we're not," said David quickly. "Mr. Blake thinks he can have the car all ready for us by morning. So we're going to be able to go on after all . . ."

David's voice trailed off into silence as Dan swung back around on his stool. Bull was forking up a mouthful of fries, and George was adding more sugar to his coffee.

Sun Ying, hurrying up to the table with a tray of steaming dishes, stopped short at David's words. "Do you think that's wise?" he asked.

"Now, Sun, don't tell me you've heard scary tales about Lost Lake too?" demanded Stewart.

Sun Ying shrugged. He began to move the dishes from the tray to the table. "Just that it has an evil reputation. Everyone knows that. I think you kids might be wise to go home and forget about it."

This is ridiculous, David thought. "Look," he said, "we inherited the place. It's ours. Do you really expect us to go home without even looking at it?"

"I guess not," said George, setting his cup down. "How long are you going to stay?"

"Oh, just overnight. We probably won't go near the lodge, haunted or not, if it's as rundown as we expect. We're not interested in that. We have all the camping gear we need. You see, Dad's a teacher and school starts on Tuesday, so he couldn't take the time, and it's too late to do anything with the property this year anyway. All I want to do is take pictures back so we can make plans for next year."

"That makes sense." Bull nodded.

George agreed. "Camp out in the open. The lake must be clean and the swimming and fishing good. What do you think, Dan?"

The officer swung back around toward them. "Yes. And you'd be wise to stay away from the old lodge itself. Evil spirits or not, it can't be safe. Nothing's been done to it for probably sixty years or more. The floors would be rotten by now. And the roof, if it's still there. I don't want to be writing a second accident report about you two."

"You won't need to, believe me," David assured him. "We won't go near the lodge. We'll probably tear what's left of it down eventually and build a cottage. But there's no hurry for that either. We like to camp."

"Well, when you're ready to build, keep me in mind." George waved away yet another refill of coffee, stood up, and handed David a business card. *George Redfern,* it said. *Builder.*

"Thank you, Mr. Redfern. As I say, it won't likely be for a year or two."

"Fine. Any time. Nice meeting you."

The builder left, rather hurriedly, David thought. The Beakhams stood up just a few minutes later.

"Now remember what we said," urged Mr. Beakham. "If the car isn't ready as soon as expected, or if it's too late when you're ready to start home, there's two rooms waiting for you."

"Thank you very much. We won't forget."

As David, Sandy, and Mr. Stewart made their way through the plates of steaming food the dining room slowly emptied, until there was only Bull left, and Dan Ketchawa, still finishing his meal.

Bull paused on his way out, before clamping the hard hat onto his head. "Take care." He grinned, indicating Dan with a slight movement of his head. "If *he* warns you about the lodge, you know you gotta take care."

"Don't worry," said David. "The ghosts are welcome to it. We won't disturb them."

Bull hesitated, then nodded again and left.

The constable rose a few minutes later. He too paused at the Stewart table. "You've had a rough day," he said. "I hope everything goes well from now on. If there's anything I can do, give me a call. And that goes for when you come back next year too."

"We appreciate that, and so will my parents." David stood up and shook his hand. "Thank you."

"Right." The man nodded, and was gone.

David turned to their host. "What do you really think of all this talk about ghosts and evil spirits?"

Stewart shrugged. "As someone said, the lodge has a bad reputation, apparently based on some old

Indian legends. If you believe in ghosts, you'll see 'em. If you don't, you won't. You ask me, it's as simple as that. I'd say Dan had the most sensible thing to say: Stay away from the lodge because it isn't safe. Camp by the lake. Swim and fish. And make use of that canoe you have on the roof of your Jeep. Forget all this nonsense. Just enjoy yourselves. Now, how about some fortune cookies for dessert?"

4

It was one of those Northern Ontario nights, Sandy thought, when the stars seem suspended just out of arm's reach in a velvet sky. She was seated on a bench in front of her room, enjoying the view of the stars, when David joined her.

"I just called Dad again," he said. "We can go on up to Lost Lake as long as the car's safe to drive. It would be a shame not to get there when we're so close. Dad says we'll worry about the body work when we get home." He sat down beside her. "What did you make of all that talk in the restaurant, Sandy?"

She wrinkled her forehead. "The people are very nice. They're awfully concerned about us, aren't they? Very solicitous."

"That's true." He hesitated. "Is that all?"

"Noooo, no it isn't. I got the impression they didn't *want* us to go to Lost Lake. Heck," she teased, "they even ran us off the road to make sure we didn't."

"I hardly think they'd go *that* far. But I got the same impression — at least about the lodge. They came up with three reasons for avoiding it." He ticked them off on his fingers. "Ghosts. Evil spirits. Rotten floors. They seemed relieved when I said we weren't interested in it."

She grinned. "Yes, and if they only knew it, only that last one is likely to deter us. The first two are more like incentives."

"Now listen," said David, "don't get any ideas. We're going to leave that lodge alone, ghosts or no ghosts. We're here for a relaxing holiday. Besides, I promised Dad we'd steer clear of it."

"So you told him all about it?"

"I told him native legends say the lodge is haunted. Dad used to teach school on a reserve, and anything to do with their legends interests him. He said if they are leery about it, we can be sure they have good reason, and that we're not to go into the lodge until he and I can go together — next year. I promised."

"He wasn't . . . alarmed?"

"No. I think it's just us, Sandy. No ordinary person would have picked up any sinister undertones in that talk in the restaurant."

"You mean we aren't ordinary?"

He shook his head. "How many people do you know who have been through two scary adventures already this summer? Not to mention being saved from death by a half-grown tree. It's just nerves, I think, pure nerves. We need to relax."

"I expect you're right. Tonight I guess I'll have to settle for a shower, but I can hardly wait to dive into that cool lake. What's the schedule for tomorrow?"

"The garage will be open at eight o'clock. I'll go see if the car's ready, and come back for you, then we'll grab breakfast somewhere before heading for Lost Lake. Okay?"

"Sounds great. But for now, I'm exhausted. Goodnight, Davie." She gave him a quick kiss. "Have a good sleep."

David walked the few steps to his room. As he turned the key he looked back at the brilliant stars studding the sky. It was a beautiful night. No time to be thinking disquieting thoughts. But they were there, in spite of his assurances to Sandy, lurking in the back of his mind.

He went into his room and switched on the TV, kicked off his shoes, and lay on the bed to watch the late news. A string of commercials preceding the news was still on when the telephone rang.

His father must have thought of something else to tell him, David decided. Who else knew where he was? He reached for the receiver. "Hello?"

A moment of silence. Then a low, husky voice. "Go home. You're not wanted here." A click, then silence.

Go home, you're not wanted here! . . . David stared at the dead instrument in his hand. Why would anyone tell him to go home? Why would they not be wanted here? It must be some stupid joke.

He replaced the receiver slowly. Perhaps the call hadn't been meant for him. Perhaps it was meant for whoever had occupied this room before him. He sat up. The telephone was an extension, so the call must have come through the office. He glanced out. There was a light in the office, someone moving around in there. Someone must have taken the call and forwarded it. He — or she — might know who had placed it.

Julia Beakham was sitting behind the desk when David opened the door to the office.

"Hello, David," she greeted him. "Is everything satisfactory?"

"Oh yes. Thanks. I just got a phone call . . ." She nodded, waiting. "But it didn't make sense. I wondered if it might have been meant for someone else. Did the caller ask to be put through to a room number?"

"No. The caller asked for the McCrimmon extension. Of course there's no one else by that name here."

"Oh." David remembered the husky voice and shivered again. "You don't know who the caller was, do you?"

She shook her head. "Haven't a clue. Didn't recognize the voice. I know a lot of people around here by voice, but not that one. Sorry." She peered up at him. "Is there . . . Can I help?"

"No, thanks. I just wondered . . ." He went to the door, paused, and looked back, but she was disappearing through the inner door.

He wandered back along the sidewalk to his room. Sandy's room had been in darkness. No sense telling her about the call until morning. And maybe not even then . . .

David turned off the TV and went to bed, but he didn't get to sleep for a long time.

5

Bill Blake saw the cigarette butt the moment he entered the office. It lay there as if challenging the NO SMOKING sign directly above it.

He hadn't smoked for years, and similar signs throughout his garage meant that few people stood around to shoot the breeze, as they did at the Esso station. That suited him just fine, as long as they brought their cars to him for repairs— which they did, because he was the best mechanic in Collinton.

He stared at the butt for another moment, puzzled. He took pride in the neatness of his garage. Things like oil stains were inevitable out in the garage area itself, but here in his office everything was clean and tidy. And that cigarette butt hadn't been there when he'd left for home the night before.

Suddenly wary, he looked around. The window

was intact, locked. The door? Its ordinary lock probably wouldn't pose much of a challenge to anyone determined to gain entry, but nothing seemed to have been disturbed. He checked the cash register. The change and few small bills he had left were still there.

He went through the door into the garage proper. Here, too, everything appeared to be in order. A quick check told him that his valuable tools were still there, all neatly stored in their appointed places, untouched. He shrugged.

The Cherokee that had been run off the road stood there, ready to go. There were plenty of minor dents still in evidence, but it would have to go to a body shop to get those looked after. He had fixed the wheel, installed a new tire, and repaired the radiator.

He raised the hood, to make sure that the hoses he'd moved to drain the cooling system were secure. They were, of course. At least from on top. It wouldn't hurt to have one more look underneath while he waited for the McCrimmon kid to show up. He pushed the button, and the hoist lifted the Jeep until its roof was close to the ceiling.

A quick look showed everything to be fine. But then a drop of something fell onto his hand. Automatically he raised it and sniffed. No, not a mixture of water and antifreeze. Something else. He frowned, reached into his hip pocket for his flashlight, and aimed it upward. There was another drop forming. Not on a hose or coupling. He frowned. It was the brake line.

"Morning, Bill." Bill Blake jumped at the sudden voice behind him. He hadn't heard anyone come in. He swivelled around.

"Oh, George, hello." George Redfern stood there, stroking his grey moustache.

"How you doing?" asked Redfern. "Hot already, isn't it? Going to be a scorcher today. Humid. That's the four-wheeler belonging to the people from Woodstock, isn't it? Is she all ready to go?"

"No, she isn't." Bill Blake turned back to peer underneath. "I don't understand it. There was nothing wrong with the brakes yesterday. I checked 'em — checked everything — thoroughly. But this morning she's leaking brake fluid. Right there." He reached up to the spot. He could feel the tiny puncture. The leak was slow, very slow, but when pressure was applied . . .

He was thinking of Gray's Hill, just north of town, with the sharp curve at the bottom, and the towering rock wall. He shivered. If he hadn't raised the car for one last check . . .

Redfern ducked under the car and followed the beam of light. "If it's that small, you could easily have missed it," he said.

Maybe some people could, Bill Blake thought, but not him. He remembered the cigarette butt.

Could it be possible. . . ?

"George," he said, "why would someone tamper with the brakes on this car?"

"Tamper! For pete's sake, Bill. Just because you missed something the first time, don't let your imagination run away with you. You're good, but you're not perfect, you know."

"I wouldn't miss *that*," Blake insisted. "I think I should contact Jeff Wilks."

Redfern laughed. "Forget it. He wouldn't believe you, and it wouldn't do your reputation any good, you know. I won't say anything, don't worry. No one will know. Here comes the owner now anyway."

David came in, wiping his brow. "Good morning, Mr. Redfern. Warm, isn't it?"

"Hot," the builder replied. "Going to be a sticky day. Could have a storm before long too."

Bill Blake came out from under the car.

"Sorry," he said to David. "I want to put in a new stretch of brake line, just to be safe. It may have been weakened. It won't take long. Could you come back in half an hour?"

"Sure. I'm glad you're being thorough. Everyone says you're the best."

"Thanks." Bill wiped his hands on a rag. "Everything else is a go. You'll be taking it to a body shop when you get home?"

"That's right. I'll go and have a coffee, and be back in half an hour."

"A coffee. That sounds good. Mind if I join you for a cup?" Redfern asked. Without waiting for David to answer he continued. "The coffee shop's right across the road. I'll be there in a few minutes." He nodded to David and jogged off down the street.

6

On the map it was labelled "Lost Road."

"Lost" was appropriate. It was unmarked, and did not appear on any map except the detailed topographical one which identified it as a "summer track." The entrance off the forest road was overgrown and easy to miss. David and Sandy had driven right by it on their first pass. But the word actually referred to the fact that it led, eventually, to Lost Lake.

The summer track plunged into valleys, then climbed up over hills to where rocks, heaved up from below, threatened to tear the oil pan off any vehicle that moved over them. It narrowed between towering outcrops of granite. It skirted the edge of an unnamed lake that flooded long sections of it. It crossed rushing streams on rickety log bridges, and ran past a spruce bog where moose stood knee-deep in water. Where it emerged into open countryside, white-tailed deer grazed on the grassy mound between the tracks, and black bears searched the nearby underbrush for berries and bugs. The track's sole advantage was its narrow width. Branches of the trees on either side could touch overhead to form a cool tunnel below.

No driver who ventured along Lost Road would turn back before reaching the end, because there was no place to do so. They would keep going, hoping to find a turning place over the next hill, or beyond the next bend, and failing every time, until they came to the top of the hill overlooking the lake.

The view there made it all worthwhile. Shaggy green-clad hills encircled a lake that shone iridescent in the sunlight. A craggy granite cliff towered at its far end, cooled by a cascade tumbling down in a rainbow mist. One rocky tree-topped island thrust up near its centre. Around the perimeter gaunt pines leaned over, their reflections caught in the surface, except where a stretch of pebbles and stones separated the water from the encroaching growth. On the far side of the lake, just visible, was the right of way where the railway builders had hacked their way into the secluded spot and out again.

Sandy and David climbed out of the Cherokee for a better view. The once-cleared land below the hills was being reclaimed by the advancing forest, but there was still evidence of a rugged garden, and what had probably been at one time a tennis court.

It took David a moment's search through binoculars to locate the lodge. It was backed up against a rocky hill, its weathered logs the same flinty colour as the age-old stone. Young trees grew around it, some towering over the gabled roof. Innumerable birds were calling and singing, dominated by the harsh voice of the blue jays and the *o-ka-ree* of the red-winged blackbird, the chattering of squirrels and the rustle of life in the undergrowth.

"It's beautiful," Sandy breathed. "It's absolutely . . . gorgeous."

David nodded. "And to think we own it. Well, some of it anyway. I'm sure the beach must have been part of the lodge property. And you can see where there used to be a tennis court."

He reached into the car for the camera and began to take a sweep of pictures that would give a panoramic view of the scene. Then he looked up. Clouds were gathering in the west. Good. They'd make it cooler. In the meantime it was hot and sultry. He wiped his brow and looked at Sandy. "What do you think we should do first?"

"Well," she said, "it's awfully warm, and that lake looks very cool. What do *you* want to do?"

"Right. I agree. Let's go."

David eased the Jeep down the last hill, following the track that led to the beach. There was still evidence of a long-abandoned flagstone walk leading from the beach to the lodge, but it was overgrown with burdocks and thistles. Beyond them he could see what must once have been the main entrance, a wide door beyond a broken-down veranda, flanked by gaping windows and topped by a crescent-shaped balcony. He remembered the suggestion that the lodge was haunted. It certainly looked innocuous enough right now, in broad daylight. But at night, in the ghostly light of the full moon?

He remembered, too, the strange telephone call. He hadn't mentioned it to Sandy, and he felt guilty about that. They seldom held anything back from each other. But this was different, he reasoned. The call made no sense. "Go home, you're not wanted here." Was "here" Collinton? If so, they had already left the town behind. Did "here" include Lost Lake? Well, they'd only be here about twenty-four hours. When they were on the way home he would tell her. Meantime, why spoil her fun?

She was out of the Jeep almost before it had stopped, kicking off her shoes, rolling her jeans up to the knees and wading out into the lake. "It's super," she called. "Not too rocky a bottom, gradually getting deeper." When the water reached her jeans she stopped. "It drops off out there a bit, I think." She turned and came back. "I'll put up the tent if you want to unload the canoe, then let's change and have a swim."

They spent almost an hour in the cool, clear water, then decided to launch the canoe so they could get a look at the lodge from a different perspective. They paddled lazily across the lake, passed the little island with its tall sentinel pines, and approached the waterfall at the eastern end. A rainbow was painted there in the dancing mist. But even as they paddled near enough to feel the cool spray on their faces the rainbow faded.

David looked up. Dark clouds were spreading across the sky, their edges beginning to blot out the sun. Overhead, they were pearl grey. In the west they were an angry blue-black. "Uh-oh!" he said. "Looks like we're in for a storm. Better head back."

"Don't I have time to swim through the waterfall?"

David hesitated. It was so stifling hot. Would there be time? But another glance at the sky decided him. "How about tomorrow? We'll come back over here before we go home."

They turned the canoe and headed back, paddling hard. With the different view of the lodge David could see an unexpected turret, and at least one other wing tacked onto the main structure. There *was* something eerie about it. He couldn't have said just what it was, but something . . . He was almost glad they wouldn't be exploring it this trip. Leave it until next spring. Leave it to brood there undisturbed and silent.

As he was looking at the tower, the sun fought free for one last time before being covered by the clouds. Rays of light moved swiftly across the water, touched the trees below the lodge, and reflected off something there, momentarily dazzling him. Something that moved.

"Did you see that?" Sandy said, just as he was about to ask her the same question. "There's something over there that caught the sun. I think — I think there's someone watching us."

Could she be right? *Was* there someone there, keeping an eye on them? Was there really something strange about the lodge, or was it just his imagination? "But why would anyone be watching us?" he said. "It's probably just something moving in the wind."

"I don't think so, Davie. Look at the lake."

"What?"

"Look at the lake. Almost no ripples. Not enough wind to move anything big, like one of those trees close to the lodge."

She was right; there wasn't much wind. In fact, everything was still, almost too still. He dug in with the paddle, ignoring the sweat running into his eyes.

Sandy looked back up at the sky, and paddled with the same urgency. Together they sent the canoe skimming back toward the beach. When the bow touched bottom they both leapt out and pulled the canoe well up onto the shore.

7

It was oppressively hot and humid now. And unnaturally still. Not a leaf quivered on the trees, not a branch moved. Not a ripple disturbed the mirror surface of the lake. Yet high above, grey, black, and dirty yellow clouds writhed across the sky.

"I don't like the look of this," David said. "We'd better get some clothes on. Then we'll take the tent down. We could be in for quite a blow."

Sandy peered back up at the high, churning clouds. "I don't like it either. Feels like a big blow's going to come, and soon." She pulled on jeans and a T-shirt over her bathing suit as David tugged on his jeans. "Back in Scotland, those kinds of clouds would look like trouble, Davie," she added, hurrying to dismantle the tent.

"I know. This sort of weather can spawn tornadoes. We'd better watch out for funnel clouds developing. Strange we didn't hear any warnings."

"Yes, but then we haven't had the radio on the whole way here from Collinton, have we?"

"No."

"Do tornadoes . . ." She stopped as a small whirl of sand lifted and moved across the beach, then subsided. Nothing else moved. Then a cedar tree nearby shivered, a shiver that started at its roots and travelled upward until the whole tree shook in the grip of some invisible power. Then it was still again. There was not a whisper, not a sign of wind anywhere else.

David caught her arm. "Look!" he hissed, pointing. Away to the north a cloud was reaching down to the earth. It was grey and broad at first, but then it gathered itself in, darkening as it did so, until it was a thin black snake, moving, striking poison fangs at the hilltop trees, then lifting, then striking again as it raced across the hill. Wherever it struck branches were stripped and flung skyward. Whole trees were wrenched out and flung aside until the air in its path was black with debris. Yet in places where it lifted back up, the trees stood untouched, unmoving. Then the entire funnel sucked back up into the spiralling clouds.

Where David and Sandy stood watching, everything was as before, deathly still. Not a sound came from the passing storm.

"There," said David, his voice unsteady, "you've actually seen a tornado. And that's as close as you want to come to one, believe me."

Sandy shivered. "Are they common up here?"

"No. Well, actually, I guess minor tornadoes are fairly common. But major ones are rare this far north. I can assure you that most of us go through life without ever seeing anything like that. I never have, before."

He sat on the collapsed tent and wiped his brow with relief. "Thank God that's over. How about something to eat?"

"Yes. Or at least a cup of tea to celebrate. Can you open the boot? The kettle's still in the car."

"Right. We'll need the stove too."

He was inserting the key into the lock when Sandy caught his arm and pointed "Look!" she whispered. "Did you ever see anything more beautiful?"

Three white-tail deer were bounding across the open space toward the trees, their fluid leaps breathtaking as they sailed over unseen objects.

David and Sandy watched them until they disappeared among the trees. "Must have been spooked by the tornado," David guessed.

"Do you know how lucky you are in Canada to have so many wild animals? I said that before, didn't I? But I can't get over how many we've seen just today. At home there's grouse and badgers and hedgehogs, and plenty of deer, but nothing like moose or bear." She had forgotten about tea for the moment. "I'm glad your game wardens protect them. Pity the elephants and rhinos in Africa that are being slaughtered just for their tusks and horns. It's dreadful!"

David frowned. "You're right. But our game wardens can't keep all the animals safe, all the time."

"You mean in hunting season?"

"No, that's pretty well regulated. But there are still deer and moose killed here just so someone can mount their antlers on a wall. Some people even have the weird idea that some animal organs will cure every disease from acne to . . . to warts. Anyway, you get the idea. And people will pay a lot to get those organs. There's millions in it for poachers."

Sandy shivered. "It's hard to believe anyone could be so ruthless. Just for money! Anyway, those deer dodged a tornado, and so did we, so let's celebrate. Oh, good. Here's the kettle."

David was kneeling beside the stove to light it when he paused, and looked up. It wasn't over yet! He knew it with a sudden tight feeling in his gut. Those ugly, churning clouds were building again. There was still something ominous in the heavy, humid air. He closed the stove lid. "Sandy!" But she had gone to the lake to fill the kettle. "We're not in the clear yet. Forget the water . . ." Alarmed by something in his voice, she hurried back.

"What is it?"

"We're still in for something." He pointed to the darkening clouds. "They haven't finished with us." He tossed the tent into the car, then the kettle and the stove.

In seconds the rain started, big, heavy drops that spattered and splashed. "Come on," said David. "We'll sit in the car until the rain passes."

The rain was hesitant at first, as if feeling out the territory like an advance guard for the torrents that were coming. They could see it now, a sheet of water approaching closer, blotting out sight of the hill as it swept down on them, moving across the clearing, wrapping around the car to cover it in a streaming flood.

David switched on the key to activate the wipers. They fought a losing battle, but David and Sandy could still see the nearby lake, now a hissing cauldron of rain and spray. The far shore was invisible. He tried the radio, to check for word on the weather, but got only static. "Guess that won't help us," he muttered.

"I didn't know it *could* rain like this," said Sandy.

"No, not much like Scotch mist, is it? It probably won't last long though." He was right. In a few minutes the rain eased up, as if a curtain had been lifted. The flooded windows cleared, but the humidity in the car was oppressive. He and Sandy left the car to wander along the old flagstone walkway toward the lodge.

"There," David said. "That's better than being stuck inside — " He stopped abruptly. He was staring past her, back in the direction from which the rain had come. "Holy smoke!"

Another tornado was coming. Not a thin, snake-like cloud this time, but a massive wall of black-ness, thundering over the hill, sweeping down into the clearing, bearing down on the lake, and on the defenceless Jeep. Small, ugly twisters shot out from its bulk, writhed and coiled and dissipated. The great boiling funnel was sucking up anything in its path, sucking and smashing and spewing out the shattered remnants of once tall trees, so that the air was black with flying debris.

For a moment they stared in terror. Then Sandy's hand was on David's arm in a vise grip. "What — what can we do? We shouldn't stay here, should we?"

Her question yanked David out of his panic. What *could* they do? He knew the proper proce-dure. Get into the basement. But what if there *was* no basement? Would a building like the lodge even have one? Or should they try to get back to the Cherokee? If the lodge was already half fallen down, maybe it wouldn't really be safe in there anyway . . .

It was the tornado's black funnel that decided

him. It loomed ever closer, ever darker, and the Jeep was farther away than the lodge. They had to make for the nearest shelter.

"Come on," he yelled, "We have to beat that monster to the lodge."

They ran, panicked. They could hear the wind behind them now, coming on their heels with the thunder and roar of an express train, fingers reaching out like tentacles to stop them and pull them back into the hungry maw of the storm.

David risked a quick look back. He saw the Jeep lifted as if it were a toy, lifted and spun around and flung into the lake. He tried to run faster, but he couldn't. As they crashed through the tall weeds and undergrowth before the veranda the hot breath of the tornado was right at their backs.

One of the veranda's rotting boards gave way, and one of David's legs plunged through, throwing him onto his face. He cried out as the jagged end tore through his jeans and into his flesh.

"Come on, Davie," cried Sandy, struggling to help him up. "We're almost there."

Almost where? he wondered. Almost into the lodge. But that tornado would tear the rickety lodge to pieces in no time. They still had to find a way into the basement, if there was one. He jerked his leg free, ignoring the pain. They smashed through an old sagging door into the gloomy interior.

Already the timbers were groaning, already there was the sound of shattering glass. At least some of the windows were still intact, David saw. But for how long?

He spun around, looking for a possible refuge. There were several doors to choose from, but no time to choose. Wind was shrieking through the open door. Something heavy thudded onto the ceiling above their heads.

Too many doors — but one possibility. Across the back of the room stood a heavy, sturdy counter that must have been the bar. Behind it were tiers of shelves that at one time held bottles and glasses, and flanked a distorted mirror.

"Come on." David staggered behind the counter, with Sandy right beside him. They crouched under it. There were shelves here and there under the counter, but still room enough for them to huddle beneath it while the lodge disintegrated around them.

They covered their heads with their arms in a vain attempt to block out the roar of the wind, the rending and crashing of timbers, the choking dust. A board, hurled across the room, smashed into the mirror, shattering it into a thousand shards that flew in all directions like a shower of arrows. Jagged chunks cut deep into the top of the counter. Tiny slivers flew out like sparks from a bonfire, biting into David's and Sandy's bare arms. The wall behind the mirror bulged, then exploded inward, exposing a crumbling room beyond. High above, the roof fell in, smashed down onto the second floor, sending huge beams crashing down onto the counter, battering it. But the counter held.

And the wind passed. Shrieking in triumph it swept on, leaving the lodge a shattered wreck.

Trembling, dazed, Sandy and David crept out of their refuge. Their faces were streaked with sweat and blood.

Sandy stared around them. "Is it over?" she whispered.

"Yes, I think it's gone. It's all over." He stayed her as she reached out her arms to him. "Just a minute. There's glass . . ." He picked a shard from her hair, another from her shoulder, carefully lifted a tiny piece from her forehead. A trace of blood left a scarlet thread down her nose and over her cheek.

"Oh. You too." She managed a smile. "Like monkeys in the zoo, looking for nits." She found a small but sharp piece piercing his T-shirt, and brushed some from his hair. Then they clung together while around them shattered timbers that had been flung together gradually shifted and settled, as if in relief that it was all over.

When at last they looked around they couldn't believe the havoc. "Davie," Sandy whispered, "it's a miracle we're alive. Look at that." A shard of glass was embedded deep in the counter, right beside where they had huddled.

"I knew we'd make it," said David, "but that doesn't mean I wasn't terrified. Well, there isn't much left for Dad to explore next spring, is there?"

At that moment came a sudden moan that rose to a shriek, then was cut off abruptly. Then utter silence. The hair on the back of David's neck stiffened. His eyes met Sandy's.

"What was *that*?"

"I don't know, but I don't think it was human. Let's get out of here!"

8

Dan Ketchawa was a little worried. Something was nagging at the back of his mind, something about Lost Lake Lodge. Sweat dripped off his chin and ran down his back as he swung his axe and the pile of split logs grew. Man, it was hot! He looked up at the ominous clouds. He'd like to finish this pile of wood before the rain came . . .

Thunk. A piece of firewood split in two. *Thunk.* Imagine those guys at the Pagoda going on about ghosts and evil spirits in Lost Lake Lodge. He set another log end-up on the stump. Ridiculous! *Thunk.* Were any of those people in the restaurant last night serious? Or were they more concerned with scaring those kids away? *Somebody* didn't want them to go to Lost Lake. But why?

There was danger there, though. Somehow he

felt that too. Rotten floorboards? Maybe, but for all he knew they were safe. He had just said that to discourage the kids from going into the lodge . . .

A helicopter beat its way overhead. He peered at it, frowning. It had been in the area for several days. How could anyone around here afford to keep a helicopter — and a pilot — on hand? he wondered. Nobody local, that was clear. And most hunters or fishermen could rent a bush plane to fly them into a campsite for less than a helicopter would cost. George Redfern used one occasionally to check on remote building sites in the surrounding area, but that would hardly pay for it being around this long. As often as George needed it, he could probably rent the one owned by CKOW anyway. Its helicopter must be a big enough expense for the radio station to carry that they'd welcome any extra revenue they could get from it . . . Anyway it had nothing to do with what was really nagging him. Someone didn't want the kids to go near the lodge — didn't want *anyone* to go near it, looked like. If that McCrimmon boy hadn't been a quick thinker, that accident could have been fatal, and he'd be at the bottom of a ravine, not up there camping with his girlfriend.

He stopped for a moment's rest. *Had* it been accidental? There had been no reason to believe that the stolen vehicle had not accidentally forced the Jeep off the road. No real clues from the tire marks, anyway. The boy had had the impression that the other driver had simply lost control, and of course if the truck was stolen the driver wouldn't wait around to see what damage he'd caused.

On the other hand, there was no evidence to the contrary either, and if the accident *had* been planned, someone was taking a big risk to keep David McCrimmon from getting to Lost Lake.

He turned, leaving the axe deep in the stump. Bill Blake had towed the Cherokee to his garage to be fixed. There was just a chance it hadn't been repaired as quickly as expected.

He jumped into his pick-up and drove over to Blake's, but a quick look in the service bay and the yard told him he was too late.

"Hi, Dan." Blake came out, wiping his hands on a paper towel. "Something I can do for you?"

"No, I guess not. I just wondered if that Cherokee that was in the accident was still here, but I see it isn't. The kids got away all right?"

"Yes. About nine o'clock, or soon after." Blake dropped the towel in a drum. "Dan," he said, "there's something been bothering me about that Jeep. In fact, I wondered if I should call you or Jeff. Now that you're here . . ."

"Yes?" Dan Ketchawa stepped closer. "What is it?"

"I could be wrong, but I'm suspicious that someone got in here and tampered with that car."

"What do you mean, 'tampered'? Are you sure?"

"No, I'm not *sure*. If I was, I'd have called you before. I suppose I *could* have overlooked a nick in the brake line . . ."

"You, Bill? Not likely. Better tell me about it."

He shook his head as he listened to Blake's story. "Okay," he muttered, "that settles it. I have to go up to Lost Lake." He headed for his truck and was pulling onto the road when his car radio crackled. He lifted it and pressed the button. "Auxiliary Constable Ketchawa."

"Dan, Jeff here. There's been a tornado. A bad one. It's practically wiped out Burns Falls. There's some dead. Lots injured. Several buildings down. I'm contacting the emergency crews, but you'll have to get up there right away to co-ordinate things."

"Shoot!" Dan Ketchawa hesitated only a moment, then pulled onto the road. The kids would have to wait.

9

"Where's the car. And the canoe? Where *is* everything?"

Sandy and David were standing on what was left of the veranda, staring out over the destruction. Some trees still stood, stripped of their branches, little more than ragged telephone poles. Others had snapped like matchwood. Still others lay with roots torn out. Branches, leaves, and pine needles were everywhere. The near surface of the lake was covered with debris.

"Holy smoke, look at the Jeep!" said David. The Cherokee had landed upright in the lake. Its hood was fully under water, but the surface reached only to the top of the rear wheels. "Looks like it ended up where the bottom slopes off. Thank God it didn't get thrown any farther, *and* that we decided to head for the lodge," he added. "I guess we aren't driving anywhere till we get a tow truck in here."

"No, but at least the things in the back will be dry — the tents, the camp stove, our clothes. We're lucky, really."

"You're right. Nothing has been damaged except the car itself, and the canoe, I guess, wherever that is."

"I suppose we'll have to walk out for help," Sandy said. "Nobody's likely to come looking for us, are they?"

"Depends on how far the tornado went before it blew itself out. And whether or not it hit any towns. If it did, I guess everyone will be too busy to worry about an uninhabited area like this. We'd better not count on anyone else, so you're right. We walk."

She nodded. "It's cooler now, thank goodness. Think we should start right away?"

"First thing in the morning might be better. That will give us a full day to get somewhere. Let's check out our gear in the car."

David rolled up his pant legs to wade out, and the cut in his leg showed, red and swollen.

"I hope the first aid kit is all right," Sandy said. "That looks nasty."

"It's really sore," David confirmed. "But it could have been a lot worse."

They started into the water, pushing their way through debris, treading carefully in case any sharp objects lay hidden under the surface. Their gear, when they checked it, was dry and intact.

They started relaying it to the beach, where they had cleared a space to set up camp. Overhead the sun shone from a cloudless sky, and a light breeze played, as if nothing had happened.

They were making the last trip to shore when Sandy stopped and pointed. "Look! There's the canoe! In that small tree."

David limped over to a spindly tree that had somehow escaped destruction. "It looks like it's okay, too. Let's see if we can get it down."

"First," Sandy ordered, "let me fix up that scrape before you get any more dirt in it. Where's that first aid kit?"

He ruffled her hair when she bent over to apply antiseptic to the cut. "I thought you had turned grey," he teased. "But I see it's just dust. Plaster dust, I suppose." She grinned up at him. Her face was smudged and streaked with dirt, and the thread of blood, but her eyes were as blue and alive as ever.

"We both need a good wash. Could we paddle over to the falls? They'd make a great natural shower."

"Good idea, *if* the canoe is seaworthy. Grab soap and towels, Sandy. And shampoo if you can find some, to get rid of this dust. We can set up camp and get something to eat when we get back."

David limped over to the foot of the tree, and tried to pull the canoe free, but it was wedged in the branches, so he had to jump to reach it. For a moment it caught, then it gave way so suddenly he had to scramble out of the way to avoid being hit.

Sandy came over with the towels. "Doesn't appear to be any damage, other than a few scratches. Let's try it in the water."

They paddled the canoe through floating boughs and debris, like an icebreaker moving through pack ice, until the water became clear again as they neared the falls.

"You want to swim, Sandy, while I see if I can find a place to beach the canoe?"

"Can't wait. Just keep hold of my towel, and toss me the soap when I need it." Sandy stood up carefully, balanced for a moment, then jumped clear of the canoe into the water with a splash that soaked David. She came up blowing.

"It's grand! Hurry up and come in." She took a deep breath and went under again.

He watched her glide under the surface toward the waterfall, then swung the canoe and headed for shore — a high cliff, really, with no landing place in sight. He spotted a ledge just above the surface, but it was too narrow, and it petered out too soon, plus there was nothing to tie the painter onto. He turned to paddle along the foot of the cliff toward the northern shore.

The remains of the lodge stood in the distance, straight ahead. The turret he had noticed earlier was still standing, but its roof was gone and its sides were gaping, like a skull's blank eye sockets. He reached for the binoculars to get a better look. He could see a staircase inside, and something else: a wire hanging down, and on the end of it something that looked like a TV aerial.

He adjusted the binoculars and looked again. No, not TV. It couldn't be. There was no TV when the lodge was in operation. There would have been radio, though. Would a radio have needed elaborate aerials back then?

He scanned the rest of the lodge. Caved-in pieces of roof. Some of the framing still standing. And something else, just visible in the tangle of trees beyond. There was no mistaking it, in spite of the fact that it was painted dark green instead of the usual bright orange. A bulldozer, or rather, a big backhoe with huge, heavy-cleated tires.

David squinted, trying to get a better look. What on earth was a backhoe doing there? Mr. Stewart had guessed that someone was taking advantage of the deserted property to fish the lake, but that didn't explain anything like this. What was going on?

And there! Was something moving, there in the wreckage? Was there someone — no, just a beam falling, if anything . . .

"Davie! Come on." Sandy was sitting on the ledge squeezing shampoo from her hair, her red curls almost brown from being wet.

"Coming." He found a narrow, pebbled beach below the hill, wide enough that he could pull the canoe half out of the water. He left the towels there, slipped into the water, and swam over to join her.

"I want to show you something," she said. She stood up, sunlight glinting off the water drops on her legs and arms, then dove into the water. She surfaced just as David stood, held his nose, leaped into the air, and hit the water with loud smack. "If a grampus saw that he'd be jealous."

"A grampus?"

"Something between a dolphin and an orca." She grinned. "Now, come on and follow me."

She swam to where the waterfall hit the surface, splashing back up into a cool mist like softly falling rain. As they drew nearer it became more dense. Then they were into the cascade itself, and it was like a stinging shower beating down on them. In a moment they were through it into a twilight world with the scarred cliff as a backdrop and the tumbling water around them, glittering in the filtered sunlight like a million jewels. There was a ledge here too, and behind it a low dark cave.

"Wow!" David stared. "Isn't this great?"

Sandy pulled herself out of the water and up onto the shelf, shaking her head so that droplets flew. "This is our place, Davie," she said. "It could be our hideout. We should give it a name."

"You're right." He was beside her on the ledge, their feet dangling in the water. "This is like a fairy's home. How about that? Could we work that into a name?"

"Maybe. But it should be in Gaelic, so no one else knows what we're talking about."

"Fair enough, as long as we use phonetic spelling — in case I want to mention it if I should ever write you a love letter. Gaelic spelling is beyond me."

She looked at him with raised eyebrows. "Do you think you might? Write me a love letter some time?"

"You never know . . ." He grinned. "Let's see now. Fairy house would be *Tie-na-shee*, wouldn't it?"

"I'm impressed! That's pretty close. But this is more than a house. Almost a cathedral. So how about *Kil-na-shee*? We don't need to be too accurate."

"Great. *Kil-na-shee* it is." He leaned back, his hands behind him on the cool rock. "This is wonderful, isn't it, the peacefulness of this place after what we just went through? It's hard to believe that one minute nature is trying to kill us, and the next we're safe in a natural cathedral like this."

"Just shows you the diversity of nature. Although I could have done without that tornado, thank you." Sandy turned to look behind them. "I wonder how deep that cave goes."

"Let's take a look later."

"How about after some food? That swim made me famished. We could make lunch, then come back later with a torch. Sorry — I forgot — a flashlight. It's pretty dark in there."

"All right, but I want to take a closer look at the lodge too. I think there's something going on there that shouldn't be. Was, anyway."

She peered over at him. "What makes you think that?"

"Well, for one thing, there's a backhoe hidden in the trees, and painted dark green as if for camouflage. Why's it here? Then there's something that's looks like a TV aerial. And that cry we heard just after the tornado — What was that? It must have been an animal, but . . ." He shifted position. "Besides, there's something I didn't tell you. I got a phone call at the motel after I left you last night. I thought it must be a hoax, or some crank, but now I'm not so sure."

"What telephone call?"

"Someone saying, 'Go home. You're not wanted here.' That was it."

"What? You're joking! Why would anyone . . . It just doesn't make sense. Why would we not be wanted here . . . Unless there's someone else who hoped to inherit the property, and resents you." She paused. "And why didn't you tell me?"

"I didn't want to worry you. I didn't really even take it seriously. Not at first. But now I'm beginning to wonder."

She was thinking back. "Before the storm, when we were paddling back to the beach, I thought for a moment I saw someone watching us. Davie, if there *was* someone there they might have been injured by the tornado."

He nodded. "I guess you're right. We'd better go see, anyway. But first we have to get back and get dressed." He put his hand on her arm. "Sandy," he said, his voice soft.

She leaned toward him. "What?"

He hesitated, then grinned. "Beat you to the canoe!"

"Dreamer!" She gave him a quick kiss on the cheek, then before he could move she was off the ledge and gone.

She beat him, hands down. She had pushed the canoe into the water and was waiting in it when he arrived. "So what's the prize for winning?" she asked.

"The winner," David said, "gets to paddle. The loser has to sit and watch."

"That sounds reasonable," she said. "But next time *I* get to name the prize. Let's go."

10

David set up the tent while Sandy fried bacon and eggs on the camp stove. The smell reminded him of the last time they had camped in northern Ontario, at Loon Lake. This time there'd be nothing like the murder they had inadvertently become involved in up there in Algonquin. Two tornadoes and one half-sunken car were enough to worry about.

As he wolfed down his lunch he hoped his suspicions about the lodge would turn out to be absolutely false . . . Well, there was a long night ahead of them, and a long walk tomorrow. In the meantime it would be better for both of them if they just kept busy.

"Davie, lunch is ready. I'm having tea. What would you like?"

"Oh what the heck," said David. "I'll have tea too."

"Really?" She looked at him wide-eyed. "There's hope for you yet. All right, tuck in."

The taste of the meal lived up to its aroma. They lingered over it while a bewildered chipmunk edged closer and chattered nervously. He was rewarded with crusts of toast.

"Now," said David when they finished, "let's go check out what's left of the lodge."

They entered by the same door as before, but were wary about rotting boards in the veranda floor, and any fallen boards or beams. Crossing the room to the counter meant climbing over more fallen wreckage and avoiding shattered glass. They passed the counter they had hidden under, then stooped through the hole in the wall into the next room. A wide, once handsome staircase mounted up into nothing, for the second floor had disappeared here. David mounted the stairs, testing each one before putting his weight on it. The tornado had been so destructive to the second floor that he could see from one end of the main lodge to the other. Only skeletons of partitions still stood, and here and there great gaps in the floor showed where the vanished roof had crashed right through.

"Careful, now," Sandy called.

"I am. Believe me, I wouldn't be up here at all if

we didn't think someone might have been in the lodge."

After a few minutes of calling "Anyone here?" he went back down, shaking his head. "Nothing — or no one — up there. I hear some noises, but I think it's just beams settling, or walls groaning. If there *was* anyone in here he wouldn't have stood a chance. Now, let's see. The way down into the basement should be somewhere around here." He peered around.

"This might be it," Sandy said. "Here, under the stairs. Through this door."

It was the door they had looked for earlier, the door to safety in the basement, when time had run out. They entered it now and went down steep steps. They could see no destruction, but nothing else either. The beam from their flashlight, and sunlight coming in from narrow windows high up near the ceiling, revealed only storerooms, emptied of everything but work tables and shelves. And dust. There was thick dust everywhere.

They walked to the far end of the room. "That's odd," said Sandy, pointing. "Look. That door has been opened recently. See, where it was pushed back, clearing the dust off the floor?"

David went closer. She was right. There was a cleared space, and then a line of thick dust where the door had stopped its arc. It must have been opened and closed again. From the inside. But there were no footprints like the ones Sandy and David were leaving everywhere they went. No one had come out.

Sandy looked at David, shrugged her shoulders, and nodded. David reached for the door handle, then pulled it open. It was a shallow closet. There was nothing inside. Not even dust.

"False alarm." He closed the door again, then turned and started back for the stairs. "How do you explain that?" he asked.

She shook her head. "The wind might have done it, I suppose, if it was on the ground floor. But down here . . . ?"

They climbed back up to the main floor and continued through the wreckage. They could guess what some of the rooms had been used for. Sagging cupboards and a rusted sink suggested the kitchen. They didn't even go into the room because it was so filled with slanted beams and caved-in walls. They decided that the big, pillared room with a view of the lake and the waterfall had probably been the dining hall, but it was also too damaged to venture into.

They were nearing what they reasoned must be the last room. They had paused in the doorway when from somewhere behind them came the noise of timbers falling. "This place hasn't finished settling yet," said David, looking around. There were still beams, all through the lodge, that could come down without warning. "There's obviously no one here. I think we should get out before more of the building comes tumbling down around us. There was an outside door back near the kitchen. Let's go out that way."

In the room they had just passed through was a gaping hole overhead, with sagging plaster-and-lathe edges. David heard a vague noise from something moving up above them.

Then suddenly there was a scream, a violent push on his back that sent him sprawling, and a jarring crash just behind him. He hit the floor on hands and knees. For a moment he didn't move, dazed by the complete unexpectedness of it. Then he looked back.

There, where a moment before he had been standing, was a huge beam. Beyond it, white faced, stood Sandy.

"Are you all right, Davie?" she asked, her voice shaking. "I'm sorry, I didn't mean to push you so hard."

"Sorry?" He said, his voice cracking. "You saved my life, and you're sorry!" He stood up slowly, picking a piece of glass from the knee of his jeans. He looked back up. It seemed safe enough overhead now . . . But then it had seemed safe enough before the roof had fallen in. He reached out a trembling hand over the beam to help Sandy.

They picked their way back to the kitchen area,

climbed over a pile of rubble, and pushed their way through a sagging door into the open air. Then David turned and caught Sandy in a tight embrace. "You saved my life!" he murmured.

"So you reward me by crushing my ribs?" she gasped.

"Sorry." He grinned. "But if you go around saving people, you'll have to expect to be hugged."

"A *hug* would be welcome. Just so I can breathe." She leaned into his chest. "That's better."

"You know," said David, after a moment, "I think those people in the Pagoda were right. We *should* stay away from Lost Lake Lodge."

She nodded against his shoulder. "I couldn't agree more. Whatever it was before, it's a death-trap now."

"Yeah. I was just wondering . . ." He was looking over her shoulder. "There's that turret at the end of the building there, but I don't remember seeing a doorway into it. Do you?"

"No. But there's nothing there anyway, you can see that." The tornado had ripped it open. They could see a stairway leading up to where a top floor should have been. Now there was nothing except the wire hanging down, with the aerial on the end of it.

"Somebody has been using it for a radio or TV," said David. "But there's no sign of anyone there now. Let's check out the backhoe."

The machine was standing behind them, on top of an abrupt rise, well back from the lodge. As they approached it they noticed a rock propped in front of one of the wheels, as if the brakes weren't trustworthy.

"What's the heck is it doing *here*?" he said. "And how would someone have got it in along Lost Lake Road? If it was driven in, we'd have noticed the tracks, or broken-off branches where the road was narrow."

"Not if it's been here for years. It looks pretty battered."

"You're right."

"Let's see if we can find where it's been used. A heavy machine like that should have left some tracks."

The tracks, when Sandy spotted them amid all the debris from the tornado, were plain, leading back through the gaunt trees. Sandy and David followed them into what had been a clearing, where a pit had been dug, and the earth piled around it. Fresh earth had been pushed into the pit as if something had recently been covered up.

"It's like a grave," Sandy whispered.

"I wish I had a shovel," David muttered. "I'd like to see what's in there."

"*I* wouldn't," she said. "I don't think I want to know. Davie, can't we leave this place *now*? Today?"

He hesitated, then shook his head. "I guess we could have, when you first mentioned it. But if we start now, night will catch us a long way from anywhere. Let's go back and decide what we want to take with us in the morning, and get it ready so we can set out as soon as it's light. Then we'll get a good night's sleep."

"I don't think *I* will," she said.

David wasn't at all sure that he would either. "Come on, if we're stuck here, how about another swim? Maybe a visit to *Kil-na-shee*?"

She brightened. "Yes, let's. Bring your flashlight so we can see how deep that cave goes."

11

"I'm going to see if I can find a place to tie the canoe the other side of the falls this time, Sandy. Closer, if possible." He dug in with the paddle. For some reason he also wanted to secure the canoe out of sight of the lodge.

"It won't do you any good," she teased. "I'll still beat you to the falls."

"We'll see about *that*," he said, though he knew she was quite right.

He swung the canoe close in so that they felt the spray from the falls, then paddled on past it. The sheer cliff continued for some distance, the rock face glowing pink in the late afternoon sun. The ledge that led in behind the falls was still visible, and in places stubborn vines pushed out from the crevices and clung to the rock face.

"Look at that," he said. "We can walk along the ledge right into *Kil-na-shee*. How about that bush there, Sandy? Think it would hold if we tied up to it?"

She reached out to tug on the gnarled vine. "Yes, it's really solid." She secured the painter to the bush and scrambled onto the ledge.

"You can walk in if you want to," she said, "but I'm going to swim." She dove cleanly into the lake, her slim form gliding under the surface toward the cascade. She surfaced below it, waved, and went under again.

He picked up the towels, their shoes, and the flashlight, climbed onto the ledge and walked along it, his shoulder now and then brushing the lichen-covered rock. It was cool now, as the afternoon waned. It probably would have been warmer in the water.

Here, close against the wall, the spray from the falls was not very heavy, but he couldn't avoid it altogether. The air was cool on his wet skin. He shivered.

Sandy was sitting on the ledge, hugging herself. "I'm getting goose bumps," she said. "Toss me one of those towels." She dried herself with one, then put on her shoes. "Ready. Let's take a quick look inside the cave, and see if it's more than just a shallow hole."

The opening was low and wide. Inside, they

could even stand up. David shone the flashlight on a high, narrow fissure leading away into the darkness. The floor beneath their feet angled off to the right, and climbed upward. The walls closed in above them, but didn't quite meet. There was a cleft up there, hidden from above by undergrowth. Then the fissure narrowed, so that there was barely room to walk single file. The floor rose abruptly and the rock closed in overhead. David hesitated, then took a deep breath, trying to shut his mind to the thought of the walls closing in on him. He had never liked closed-in places much.

He dropped to his knees and crept forward, but in a moment he saw daylight ahead. Seconds later he was pushing a leafy sumach out of the way, and emerging onto a hillside. "We have a back door to *Kil-na-shee*," he said. "I bet no one has ever been in there before."

Sandy clambered through the bush behind him. "You could be right," she agreed. "The opening's well hidden, and why would anyone come this way anyhow?" She looked around. The trees here were still standing tall, untouched by the passing tornado. "The lodge must be over there, beyond the hill. Right?"

"Yes. We could take a look now, except we're hardly dressed for it. Let's go back, and build a campfire."

*   *   *

84

The sun sank behind the western hills, spreading fire through a rack of clouds. The lake reflected the sunset for a few moments, then a leaden grey veil was pulled over its surface. Darkness began to gather in the depths of the valley. The waterfall hung like a fragment of lace, then disappeared into the deepening shadows. The lodge, a misshapen form lurking at the foot of the hill, receded into the gloom. Night took over.

The campfire tossed glowing sparks into the air. Nearby, in the rushes by the water's edge, bullfrogs began a resonant chorus, and far away the howl of a lone wolf hung on the air, then died away.

"Davie," said Sandy, "you're awfully quiet. What are you thinking about?"

David turned to her. "A couple of things that make me wonder." He ticked them off on his fingers. "The reputation this place has for being haunted. A strange telephone call, telling us we're not wanted. That TV aerial. The backhoe that looks intentionally camouflaged. Your impression that we were being watched. A cupboard that must have been opened from inside, yet no one came out and no one was in there. A beam that fell and almost killed me. You know, I *might* have seen some movement up there before that happened, but I can't be sure it wasn't just another beam shifting because of what the tornado did. And there's one other thing I've begun to wonder about. I think we might have been run off the road on purpose."

"Run off? You think that wasn't an accident?"

"Let's just say I'm suspicious because of all the other things that have happened. Something is — or was — going on here, and we're not supposed to know what it is."

She was silent for a moment. "So, what do you think we should do, tell the police when we get out of here? They may think we're just crying wolf, you know. There could be a reasonable explanation for everything."

"You're right. *Maybe* there is, but I don't think so. Anyway, if you still want to leave first thing in the morning, that's what we'll do."

"Come on, Davie. You have something else in mind. What is it?"

"Well, we could stay. Not here, but in *Kil-na-shee*. We could head out along Lost Road in the morning as if we're going home, in case someone's watching us. But when we're out of sight we'll circle round and get into our cave by the back door. Then we'll spend the day keeping an eye on the lodge. If there's anyone there he's bound to show himself once we've left. Then maybe we can find out what's going on."

"But if there's someone there, where was he when we went through the lodge?"

"Oh there's plenty of places he could have been. Remember when I went up the stairs? I could see from one end of the building to the other, but there were still a few partitions standing, especially in the corners. He could have been behind one of those. He could even have dislodged that beam that almost hit me. And I don't think we went through the whole building. I remember seeing a wing at the far end from the lake when we were out in the canoe." He shook his head. "We didn't go through any wing, did we?"

"Hard to tell with all the damage, but I don't think so. We checked every door, though, didn't we? How would you get into the wing?"

He hesitated. "That cupboard, Sandy. I keep coming back to that. Maybe we should have examined it more closely. We decided someone opened it from inside, but didn't come out. Therefore he must have stayed inside. But he wasn't there. So what does that leave us?"

"A false wall in the cupboard! A hidden door! That must be it."

"I think so too."

"Then let's stay, Davie. You know what we could do? We could take some stuff — food, and the camp stove — over to *Kil-na-shee* tonight. It's very dark. No moon." She looked up. "And no stars showing through the clouds. No one could see us out on the lake tonight. What do you say?"

"Good idea. I'll get some things ready."

*   *   *

Deep in the shadows beyond the circle of light thrown by the fire, they pushed the canoe into the water and headed out into the black night. David steered straight out into the lake, then veered a little to the left. Somewhere out there was the island. They found it, a blacker shadow, its towering pines barely distinguishable against the dark sky. They skirted it and steered toward where the cliff must be, and before long they could hear the waterfall tumbling into the lake.

They found the ledge and the mooring bush, more by feel than by sight, and transferred the well-filled backpack and camp stove into the cave, getting only slightly wet in the process.

They had started back, with muffled paddles, when they saw the brief, unmistakable beam from a flashlight. It came from the shadows beyond where the lodge would be, swept over the backhoe, and vanished. There was no further sign of life.

David took a deep breath, and let it out slowly. "Did you see that?"

"I saw. So now we know for sure. Someone *is* there."

"Right. Still want to carry on as planned?"

"Yes."

There was a hint of excitement in that single word. David nodded to himself. He'd had no doubt, really, that she would be anxious to stick with their plan.

Their campfire was a circle of dying embers when they reached it again. They decided to let it die, and try to get some sleep.

Sandy disappeared into the tent. David followed her a few minutes later and crawled into his own sleeping bag without disturbing her, but he lay awake, listening to the night sounds. The frogs kept up their chorus, an owl hooted, and loons sounded their eerie call from far out on the lake.

David had no idea of the time — his watch hadn't survived the tornado — when he gave up the idea of sleep, and crept back outside. It was dark, darker than ever, it seemed. He walked down to the shore, where the water lapped gently on the pebbles, a soft, drowsy murmur. He followed the shoreline along to the reeds. The frogs went silent for a moment, then paid him no attention. He turned away from the lake. Somewhere up ahead was the lodge. He walked toward it, looking for some sign of movement there, but all was blackness.

He couldn't have said what it was that caused the first sudden jolt of terror. A sound, maybe, more felt than heard; a movement, something intangible in the utter darkness. But he knew there was something, something huge and nameless, bearing down on him out of the night.

And on the tent where Sandy lay sleeping.

A moment frozen in panic, then he was running, stumbling, screaming.

"Sandy! Sandy, get out! Hurry!"

He heard it now. Something crashing through the debris left by the tornado, right on his heels. Close behind him now, towering over him. At the last moment he flung himself aside. A huge black shape rushed past him, crushing the remains of the campfire, flattening the tent like so much paper. It hit the lake with a shattering splash.

"Sandy!" he cried.

"Davie! I'm all right!" She was there, a shadow running out of the darkness, flying into his arms. "Oh Davie! What *was* that?"

For a moment he couldn't answer. He hung onto her while the horror subsided and his heartbeat started to slow a little.

"The backhoe," he said, still unbelieving. "Oh God, Sandy! I thought you were still in the tent. I was afraid . . ." He couldn't put into words what it was he feared.

"I heard you get up and go out, so I got up to join you. And then that thing rushed past. Was anyone driving it?"

"I couldn't tell, but the motor wasn't running. It was just rolling down the hill."

The backhoe was a black hulk now, half buried in the water.

"It was parked on that hill up near the lodge," he said. "Remember there was that stone — that big one — in front of the wheels? To keep it from moving. I guess the brakes weren't dependable."

"Then someone must have moved that stone. Someone who hoped it would hit the tent. With us inside." She shivered. "A few minutes earlier we would have been, too."

They stood close together, there in the blackness. "Well," said David at last, "he must know he failed if he heard me yelling for you, so he knows we're alive. So now what? It's still a long time until dawn. What else can he try? I think he's run out of 'accidents' by now."

"Well, what would we do if we thought it *was* an accident — no sense letting him think we suspect anything. Put the tent back up and go to sleep?"

"Probably, but you won't get me back in a tent tonight — even if that thing didn't rip it to shreds. Let's just see if there's anything left of the sleeping bags, and sleep out in the open."

"All right. We can take turns keeping watch, just in case. Have you got your flashlight?"

"Not any longer. I left it in the tent. I expect it's flatter than a pancake. How about yours?"

"I think I left mine in the canoe. Let's go see."

They walked together, neither willing to go beyond hand's reach of the other, to where the canoe had been pulled well up onto the beach. Sandy found her flashlight and pressed the switch. The beam swung round in a wide arc as she moved it back along the track the backhoe had made as it smashed though the debris. Aimed the other way, it showed the flattened tent, and beyond that, the backhoe itself, stranded like a half-beached whale.

They pulled the sleeping bags, badly ripped but still usable, out of the tent.

"Let's put them over there," David suggested, "well away from here. Better put out the light, too, so if anyone's watching they won't know where we are." They found a spot near the water, free of branches and other debris from the storm, and laid out the sleeping bags side by side.

"You go first, Davie," Sandy said. "Right now I'm too wide awake to sleep anyway. If I get drowsy I'll waken you. Okay?"

"Not sure if I can sleep either, but I'll try." He slipped into his sleeping bag and lay there, one hand out, holding on to Sandy's. Eventually, he slept.

12

When dawn came, creeping across the sky and melting the darkness, Sandy was on the shore, hugging her knees, a sweater over her shoulders. David was asleep.

She watched the backhoe take shape. It looked harmless enough now, with water lapping around it. A little farther out in the littered lake was the Cherokee, its back end sticking up in the air. She turned to look at the lodge. It was emerging out of the shadows, battered, seemingly lifeless. She shivered.

She rolled up her jeans, took off her shoes, and waded out to the car. If anyone was watching, she and David would be expected to take a backpack with them when they set out on the long walk to the main road. She reached the Jeep and began to stuff odds and ends into the second backpack, anything that was light and bulky. When she turned to go back to shore, David had crawled out of his sleeping bag and was watching her, yawning.

"Did you see the binoculars anywhere?" he called. "I think I left them in there."

"No. Just a minute. I'll take another look." A moment later she was wading ashore, holding them up. "Got them. Did you sleep well?"

"Like a baby, knowing you were watching over me. But I'm beginning to think we should have kept the camp stove here. I'm hungry."

"We could build a fire," she suggested. "There's oatmeal here, and tea bags. What more do we need?"

"A breakfast fit for a highlander," quipped David. "I suppose we have to assume that someone is watching us, so we should act as if we're preparing to set out on a long walk. We wouldn't do that without a hearty breakfast, right?"

"Right! Tea and porridge coming up." It didn't take long to light a crackling fire and set the oatmeal bubbling and the kettle boiling. David sat cross-legged across from Sandy, where he could watch the lodge without being obvious. Was there someone there, in the shadows where the door used to be? Maybe. Someone motionless, watching them? He couldn't be sure.

"Sandy," he said, "Don't turn your head, but I

think we're being watched. There could be someone standing in the doorway. I want to check with the binoculars, but that would be a dead giveaway. I need some sort of excuse."

"No problem." She winked at him. "Look!" She stood and pointed away over to the north where a gap-toothed line of trees crested the hill. "That bird! What is it?"

"What bird? Where?" On cue he picked up the glasses and followed her pointing finger. "I see a hawk . . ."

"No, not that one. There. See? It's flying toward the lodge."

"Yes! I see it!" He stood up, scanning the entrance to the lodge as he pretended to follow the erratic flight of a bird, then swung the binoculars back up into the sky. A moment later he lowered them and sat down.

"I've no idea what that bird was. Probably the invisible sapsucker," he whispered. "But there's definitely someone watching us." He raised the glasses again, this time looking out over the lake, pointed in that direction, then handed the glasses to Sandy. "Your turn to look at an imaginary bird," he said.

"Aye, all right. I'll play along."

* * *

Half an hour later they stowed everything they wouldn't need in the back of the Cherokee.

David hoisted the pack to his back. "Let's go over that hill at the west end of the lake, till we're out of sight of the lodge, then decide the best way to go."

A wide swath of destruction marked the path of the storm. It had raked down from the northwest, obliterating much of the trail that had been Lost Road, so there was little point trying to walk out that way. The main front had roared over the hill and across the valley, smashing the lodge, then sweeping over the hill behind it. Only the outer edge had brushed the lake. The trees on the island remained untouched, and on the far side of the lake there was nothing to indicate that a tornado had passed nearby. The old rail line right-of-way lying along the lake's southern shore was clear and level.

"I wish we could walk along *that*," said Sandy. "But I'm afraid we might be seen from the lodge."

"But only for the first bit," David pointed out. "See, farther along there's a line of trees hiding the track. We'll have to stick to the bush on the far side of the line for a start, but when we get as far as those trees we can come out and walk along the line. No one will see us then."

It was a long walk around the lake, but the morning remained cool, and they made good time once they reached the abandoned railway embankment. At one point a rushing stream plunged through a narrow cleft almost fifteen metres deep.

Many of the support timbers in the trestle bridge that crossed it were missing. So were some of the ties that had held the rails in place. Through the wide gaps they could see the water below seething over hidden rocks. But there were weathered planks laid across the widest gap. They tested the planks, and reassured, crossed without mishap. The other gaps could be jumped over easily enough.

The right-of-way was climbing now, in a long, easy grade, the lake dropping away below them. Then they came to the place where the railway builders had had to blast a narrow canyon through the unyielding granite. Sandy and David left the line here and scrambled up the hill that towered over the eastern end of the lake, directly above the falls.

The terrain was rolling with glens and hills, but each valley was shallower, each hill higher, so that they were always climbing. Here and there were open spaces, with sumachs splashing their late summer colour along the slopes.

David stopped, reaching his hand out for Sandy's. "Which is our sumach?"

"Oh. I don't know," she admitted. "We should have looked for some landmark so we'd recognize it."

"We'll do that this time — once we find it."

"That one could be it." She was pointing. "It was on a slope like that." Her hand dropped. "Or it could be that next one. I remember seeing another sumach off to the right like that. You check one and I'll go on to the next."

She found it on the third try. "Eureka, Davie," she called, parting the branches to disclose the dark, narrow passage.

"Good!"

When he joined her at the opening she was pointing up to where a ledge of rock jutted out above them. "We won't have any trouble next time," she said. "We'll just look for that."

"Reminds me of The Beak," David grinned. "If we ever have to look for it again we'll just think of Mr. Beakham."

Sandy lowered herself into the opening. David crawled in backward behind her, to make sure the branches of the sumach would appear undisturbed. When the cleft widened and the roof lifted he stood and turned to follow her, scrambling through the fissure until they came to the ledge, where daylight filtered through the curtain of tumbling water.

A thin veil splashed at the edge of the falls where they would have to take up their post to watch the lodge, not heavy enough to hinder their view, but enough to get them wet.

"We'll have to put on our swimsuits," Sandy said. Hang on a minute while I change." She disappeared into the darkness of the cave.

David turned the glasses toward what he could

see of the lodge. There was something different about the aerial. It wasn't hanging loose any more.

Sandy, back now in her silver swimsuit, took the glasses from him. "You can change now," she said. "I'll holler if I see anything."

"Okay."

He was pulling up his trunks when she called.

"Davie, come quick! There's someone —"

"Just a minute." He joined her and reached for the glasses.

"Look. See the man there? You know who it is?"

"Do I know . . . ? How would I know anyone around here? Darn!" The lens was wet, distorting his view. He turned to reach for his shirt and used it to wipe the lens dry. Yes, there was the man, a big man with jeans held up by wide red suspenders, a baseball cap on his head. "Hey! It's the big guy — what's his name? Bull! What's he doing here?"

"He must have driven out here for some reason."

"Then where's his car?"

"Behind the lodge maybe?" Sandy suggested.

"No, I think we'd have heard it, though with the noise from the falls, who knows? Anyway, Lost Road's all torn up. He can't have driven. What *is* he doing here?"

"I don't know. Making sure we don't go into the lodge, I'll bet. That seemed to be what had everyone so worried."

Bull was walking toward their former campsite.

They watched him kick at the ashes of their morning fire, then wade out into the lake without bothering to remove his shoes or roll up his pants. He peered into the windows of the Cherokee, turned back to the shore, stood irresolute for a moment, then began to climb the hill in the same direction they had gone.

David wiped the lens on his shirt again and handed the glasses back to Sandy.

"*He's* going to have to walk out of here too," he said. "Not even a four-wheel drive is going to get through all that stuff that's clogging Lost Road. I hope he goes soon. That'll give us lots of time to have another look at the lodge."

"He's not leaving though," Sandy said. "He's coming back." Bull had paused at the top of the hill, looked around for a long moment, then started back down.

"Well, he saw the damage. He knows he can't get out by car. I'll bet he's going back to call for help. Ten to one he has a radio transmitter somewhere in the basement of the lodge. The aerial has been repaired."

"But what kind of help can he expect? He'll have to walk —" She stopped, listening.

Bull had stopped, and he was looking up.

Then David heard the sound too. "A helicopter!" The unmistakable sound of the motor and the beating of the blades was coming closer.

"Do you suppose someone's coming at last to check out the damage from the tornado?"

"Could be. They'll be flying along the storm path to make sure no one's been hurt. I wonder how Bull will explain his presence here."

"He doesn't seem worried, anyway." Sandy was still watching him through the binoculars. "He's just standing there waiting."

David tensed. "I just had a thought. Suppose Bull radioed for help first thing this morning, and this is his help coming now. If so, no wonder he isn't worried."

For a moment Sandy was silent. "I think you might be right. He's waving."

The helicopter came into view, sweeping around in a wide circle, banking steeply. Then it straightened up and settled on the beach. A man descended, ducking low beneath the slowing rotors.

Sandy handed the glasses to David. "Here we go again," she said. "*Another* acquaintance from the restaurant."

"You're kidding. Who is it this time?"

"The man who took all night to drink one cup of coffee."

"Well, what do you know," muttered David, focussing the glasses. "Mr. George Redfern. I met him again yesterday, did I tell you? He was at the garage when I went to pick up the car. I had coffee with him while I was waiting. He drinks coffee a lot faster in the morning."

"Do you suppose he's part of whatever it is that's going on?"

"Looks like it. It also looks like he expected to find Bull here. And they'll be taking off in a minute." He lowered the glasses and looked at Sandy, frowning. "Sandy, we're not going to have much time to explore the lodge after all."

"That's just what I was thinking. When Bull takes off in that helicopter he'll expect to see us walking back to Collinton. When he doesn't, he might get suspicious and come back."

"We have to move fast. Just pull on your clothes over your swimsuit and let's see what they're going to do."

He took one last look through the binoculars. The two men were conferring. Bull pointed to where Sandy and David had disappeared over the hill, then he and George Redfern climbed into the helicopter.

"Okay," said David. "Let's go."

13

A few minute's walk from *Kil-na-shee*, they were again in the havoc left by the tornado. Sandy and David had to climb over fallen trees and around huge exposed roots, and scramble through snarled and tangled branches to approach the lodge from the rear. As they fought their way down the hillside behind the lodge, David paused and pointed.

"See the aerial? It leads down into that room, but there's obviously nothing left in there. It must go right through to the basement. We have to get in there somehow. And I think the way in must be through that cupboard."

Sandy nodded. "We came to a dead end wall. The only door went into the cupboard, so I think you're right."

They reached the lodge at last, skirting the rear

wing above which the battered tower loomed.

"There must be a door into the wing from the main floor too," Sandy reasoned. "I guess we just didn't go far enough. I don't see any exterior door. Let's go in by the kitchen entrance, this way."

They entered the devastated building again, climbing over rubble to reach the door under the stairs. Testing each stair to make sure it would hold, they picked their way down to the basement.

"Look," whispered Sandy, "Those are our footprints coming and going. Just ours. No one else has come this way."

David nodded. They followed the footprints to the end wall. The door was still closed, the telltale arc of dust-free floor still visible. He opened the door.

Once again they stood in what appeared to be an empty cupboard. "Okay," he muttered, "there's got to be a way out of here. *Another* way." The back wall of the cupboard was of close fitting horizontal boards. David pointed to some faint markings. "There used to be some shelves there. Removed for some reason. But there's obviously no door. And that end's got to be the outside wall. So it must be this end." He swung his light. The boards here were vertical. And just above head height was a horizontal line.

"There!" he said. "Someone's cut a door out of this wall. Four boards wide. But there's no hinges this side, so it must open out. And no knob or anything. There must be one on the other side." He pushed tentatively. The boards gave a little.

"Something's holding it," he muttered. "Probably just a hook." He removed his knife from its sheath, inserted it between two of the boards and drew it upward. It struck some object. A quick jerk up and the object gave way. The door swung outwards.

They were in a hallway. At the end was a narrow staircase, leading up to the main floor where a windowed door opened into the tower. There was another door on the right. He put his hand on the doorknob and stopped, listening. "Hear that?"

She nodded. "It sounds like a motor of some kind, doesn't it?" She sniffed and made a face. "That smell! What is it?"

"I don't know." He hesitated another moment, then edged the door open.

They were in a small room with some kitchen cupboards, an electric stove, a refrigerator, a small TV and, in the corner, a radio transmitter. An unmade day bed was against one wall.

"Someone has been making himself right at home in your great-uncle's building, hasn't he?" whispered Sandy.

David nodded. "I wonder . . . " He opened the refrigerator door. The light came on, revealing well-stocked shelves. "That explains the noise," he said. "It must be a gas-driven generator, in through there somewhere. But what's someone doing here? A lot more than fishing in the lake, that's for sure."

"It looks as if a caretaker stays here. Or a security guard, something like that. There must be something beyond that door — Davie!" She caught his arm and pointed to the floor. "Those stains!" Several reddish brown splotches marked the floor, boot size, leading from an inner door. "There's a stain like that on the floor in Holyrood Palace," she said, a catch in her voice. "It's been there for hundreds of years. They can't get rid of it. It looks like this, except this is darker. That means it's fresher." She looked up into David's face. "It's blood."

He gulped. He had a sickening feeling that she was right. "Maybe it is. We have to find out." He approached the inner door, then paused again, his hand on the knob. There was a new sound from the other side, a strange whimpering like a frightened child.

He glanced at Sandy. "Well, here goes." He opened the door.

They were in a scene from a horror movie. Dried blood smeared the floor and a butcher's block. More had drained into a gutter. There was blood dripping from the mutilated carcass of a black bear hanging on a meat hook. At the back, in a squalid cage, two bear cubs paced and whimpered.

"Oh no!" Sandy clutched David's arm.

He stared around, red-faced with anger. A big chest freezer stood in one corner, and in another a pile of stag and moose antlers were tangled in a stack against the wall. He opened the freezer. It was packed with neatly wrapped packages, each with its own label. Bear Gall Bladder. Bear Paws. Bear Testicles. Stag Liver. He had seen enough. Seen too much. He closed the lid, sickened. "It's — it's what we were talking about, killing animals for their body parts. And for the money, of course. Lots of it. Probably millions of dollars . . ."

Sandy was ashen-faced. "I never dreamed anyone would do this."

"It started with gall bladders, I think. But I guess poachers persuaded gullible people that other body parts were just as effective, or potent, maybe." He pointed to the antlers. "I've read that they grind those into powder and sell it as an aphrodisiac in countries like China, but other places too, I guess. There's millions in it, Sandy. Millions. No wonder they didn't want us to find this."

"I can't . . . I can't believe people would do this kind of thing."

"Believe it," he said, grimly. "It's staring us in the face."

"But those poor little cubs. Why haven't they killed them too?"

"I don't know." The door into the cage was secured only by a metal pin through a clasp. Part of a fish lay on the floor. "They're feeding them, see? So they must be keeping them alive for some reason. And you can be sure it must be worth their while. Maybe they're going to sell the cubs to some sleazy little zoo or circus. Some people would pay big money to get hold of a bear cub. To put on show, or to train to do some stupid tricks."

"Let's get out of here. If we stay any longer I think I'm going to be sick."

"That makes two of us."

They turned and went out through the little anteroom into the hall. "Wait," Sandy said. "What about the cubs? We should at least set them free."

They were about to turn back when the sound of a helicopter stopped them in their tracks.

"They're back," she whispered. "We've got to get out of here before it's too late."

David looked around quickly. "They can't be sure we're here. They're just afraid we *might* be. If we can find a place to hide they'll likely go away again."

"Back among the fallen trees behind the lodge," she suggested. "There's lots of places to hide there if we can make it." The noise of the helicopter had stopped. "It must have landed! Quick!"

The way out through the cupboard would take them back into the main part of the lodge. "We'd better find another way out," said David. "This way! Through the tower . . ."

They raced up the rickety stairs to the base of the tower. There was no need to find a door. The tornado had ripped great holes in the walls for them to climb through. They were at the back of the lodge now, an open space of only a few metres separating them from the devastated forest.

"Just a minute," said David. "Let's take a quick look."

He crept along the battered wall of the tower, Sandy close behind, until they could look the length of the lodge. The helicopter was sitting near their former campsite, its rotors blurring to a stop.

"Hey!" exclaimed David. "It's not the same helicopter!"

Sandy joined him. "You're right. Can you make out those letters on the side?"

"CKOW!" David grinned triumphantly. "It's Walter Stewart. Come on, Sandy, we're saved!"

14

"David! And Sandy!" Walter Stewart held out his hands. "Thank God you're alive." His grip made them wince. "When we discovered that the tornado had veered this way we feared the worst. And when we saw the Jeep in the lake and no sign of you . . . What happened?"

"We saw it coming in time to get to the lodge."

"But the lodge is a wreck. You're lucky it didn't fall down and bury you."

"We tried to find the way to the basement, but there wasn't time. Luckily there's a big sturdy counter in what must have been the bar. We got under that, and I guess it saved our lives. Did the tornado do much damage anywhere else?"

"Plenty. That's why we weren't here sooner. It practically wiped out a little village called Burns

Falls. Three people died and a dozen or so were hospitalized. Thank goodness the tornado blew itself out before it reached any larger centres. I couldn't believe it when I saw that backhoe in the lake. The tornado did that?"

"No. Mr. Stewart, listen. We've stumbled onto something pretty serious here. Remember when we were in the restaurant with you, and some people advised us to stay away from the lodge?"

"Oh, you mean the nonsense about it being haunted. You don't mean there's something to it?"

"Not really, but back there at the far end of the lodge, down in the basement, there's a dead bear and a freezer full of animal body parts. And a pile of antlers. You know what they do with those."

Stewart was frowning, his face drawn. "Oh yes, I know all about that business. But I thought you said you didn't make it to the basement."

"Well, we were pretty sure there was someone here. For one thing, we spotted a TV aerial. That certainly wasn't here in Uncle David's time. And we thought we saw some movement, someone watching us. So after the tornado passed we thought we'd better go through the building in case there was someone in there who'd been hurt. We didn't find anyone at first, and we had to get out because some of the rafters were still falling. We followed the backhoe tracks to a pit that was being filled in and covered over. Now we know what that must be." He looked at Sandy. "It's where they bury the carcasses."

"But how did the backhoe get into the lake?"

"I'm coming to that. In the middle of the night someone removed the stone — there was one under the wheels to hold it in place, and it rolled down the hill right over our tent. If we'd been in it . . ."

"You mean . . . !" Stewart's eyes went wide. "Now just a minute. Are you sure it wasn't accidental? Maybe the stone was too small to hold it, or it shifted when the tornado went through."

"It wasn't accidental," David insisted. "And what we've discovered since convinced us. This morning we pretended to go away, climbing over the hill toward Lost Road like we were going to walk out, in case someone was watching us. Then we circled around the lake and came up behind the lodge, and hid there and watched. We saw a man come out, one of the men who had been in the restaurant. The big man you called Bull."

"Bull? Bull Corrigan?" Stewart whistled. "What did he do? Where did he go?"

"A helicopter came down and another man we recognized met Bull. It was George Redfern."

"George Redfern!" The man nodded, still frowning. "He took Bull away, did he?"

"Yes. So then we went back into the lodge for a thorough search. That's when we found the bear, and the freezer full of body parts."

"All right. This is serious business. You'd better take me to see it." He turned to give some instructions to his pilot while Sandy and David waited impatiently. "Okay. Lead the way."

15

"It's in through there." They had passed through the cupboard and entered the anteroom. David pointed to the inner door. Beyond it they could hear the whimpering of the cubs.

"You'd better show me."

"I'll wait here," said Sandy. "I've seen enough."

"No," said Stewart. "I think it's better if you come along."

She looked at him in surprise, then shrugged and followed David. Stewart followed the two of them in, closed the door, and stood with his back to it.

"Take a look," said David, pointing. "That freezer is full of packages, all labelled . . ."

His voice died away. Something was the matter with Walter Stewart. He wasn't looking at the freezer, or the carcass of the bear impaled on the meat hook. His face was no longer friendly. It was frozen, as if a mask had been pulled down over it.

David tried to read the man's eyes. He's shocked at what we've shown him, and so he should be. But then David knew, with terrible certainty, that he was wrong. That he and Sandy had made a critical mistake.

"There's an old saying." Walter Stewart's voice was deliberate. "Maybe you've heard it. It goes like this: 'Three can keep a secret — if two of them are dead.'"

David felt Sandy's hand creep into his, and clutch it. He tried to laugh, and failed miserably. "What do you mean?" But he knew very well what Walter Stewart meant.

"It should be obvious. There are three of us here, sharing a secret. A secret worth millions of dollars. And I fear that whoever coined that saying was quite right. Three *can* keep a secret, but only if two of them are dead."

"Then you are a part of this . . . this . . ." Sandy couldn't go on.

He nodded. "Oh yes. And I have no intention of letting you or anyone else interfere with my operation. We tried to warn you to stay out of the lodge. We knew we would have to move out sooner or later when old man McCrimmon died, but as long as you could be persuaded to stay out of here for the present, we would have all winter to find another place and make the move. And now thanks to the tornado and your damned curiosity you know too much. Two are going to die, and I assure you *I'm* not going to be one of them."

"But that's crazy." Sandy shot back. "There must be more than three of you in on this."

"Oh, of course. Counting our people in Toronto there are maybe twenty of us. But let me assure you that there are twenty of us who will keep the secret because our wealth depends on it, not to mention our freedom. So we'll change the quotation if you like: Twenty-two can keep a secret, if two of them are dead."

"You can't expect to get away with this," David said, trying to steady his voice.

Stewart shrugged. "The tornado will be blamed for your deaths. Two bodies in a shattered building won't be all that surprising when people see the other wreckage around here. Oh, we'll get away with it all right."

He turned abruptly, went through the door and closed it behind him. They heard the *click* as he set the lock.

While they stood in stunned silence, hand in hand, they heard him cross the other room, then the sound of the second door closing. No doubt the lock was set on that one too.

"How does he mean to kill us?" Sandy asked. "He

can't shoot us, even if he has a gun. That would alert the police. It will have to look as if we've been crushed under the beams."

"So that's what they'll try, I guess," muttered David. "But we're not going to stand around and let them, that's for sure."

"No!" said Sandy. "We didn't escape two tornadoes and that backhoe to die here. Someone's looking after us, Davie. As always. We have to figure out how to get out of here."

They looked around the room. There were two windows high up, but they were mere slits to let in the daylight. No escape that way. There was the ugly carcass, blood still dripping onto the floor. There was the blood-spattered butcher's block, and several meat cleavers hanging on hooks above it. There was a band saw — used, they supposed, to cut bone. And the freezer with its grisly contents. The pile of antlers. The two bear cubs were silent now, crouched together at the rear of the cage.

David turned to the door. It was panelled, but obviously solid. The hinges? No luck there either. The bolts were on the other side. He took another look around. Nothing but solid walls backed by solid ground, except for the narrow slits where the windows were. It would have to be the door. But how...?

"Those things," cried Sandy, pointing. "Meat axes. What do you call them? Cleavers!" She reached over for one of them.

David hesitated. "They'll hear us, and come running."

"But there's no other way, is there?"

"No." He grabbed the other cleaver. It was heavy and sharp. He swung it back and down. It crashed into the door's upper panel, cutting a jagged split up its length.

"It's coming," Sandy said. "Let me have a go."

Taking turns they attacked the door, hacking at it with the cleavers. The noise was deafening, but there was no time to worry about that. Finally the panel gave. David reached through to turn the lock. The battered door swung open.

"Just a moment." Sandy turned and went back to the cage. She pulled the pin to open the door. The cubs, still cringing, stared at her. They didn't move. "Come on, little fellows," she urged. "Follow us." She didn't wait to see if they obeyed.

Another door, the same kind, stood between them and the hallway. They didn't hesitate this time. There was no sign of Stewart or the others. Not yet. But their escape attempts must have been heard. There was no time to lose.

They attacked the second door. It resisted stubbornly, wasting precious minutes, but finally they could reach through to open it. At the end of the hallway were stairs leading up to another door. Beyond that was the tower. The cupboard was there too, but that would take them back into the basement proper and up into the middle of the lodge. Too dangerous. The door leading out into the tower had a window. No trouble there, even if it was locked. Through it they could see, beyond the tower, the shambles of the forest. Plenty of places to hide there.

They ran toward the door until David stopped, clutching Sandy.

"There's something wrong," he whispered. "This is too easy. Stewart must have seen those meat cleavers. Why did he leave them? They must have heard that racket we made breaking down the doors. Why didn't they come and stop us?"

Sandy went white. "They expect us to escape! They're waiting out there for us — "

A noise behind them. They jumped, spun around.

The bear cubs had followed them. They stood at the foot of the stairs, sniffing freedom, but suspicious.

"Poor little things," whispered Sandy. "We won't let you be killed. Come on, Davie. Let's open the door and let them go."

The cubs seemed to sense her urgency. They scrambled awkwardly up the stairs. The moment David opened the door the cubs shot past him.

A huge crash. Thick beams, meant for Sandy and David, slammed down.

"Oh no!" cried Sandy. "What have we done!"

"It's all right. Look." David pointed to the settling beams. "Those would have done us in, but they landed on the rubble and the cubs scooted right under them! And *we'd* better make our break too. Come on," he yelled. "Now!"

They dashed through the door, mindless of everything but the opening in the outer wall, ignoring the shouts behind them. They climbed over rubble, reached the opening, leapt to the ground, and were running, running for the shelter of the fallen trees.

When they reached them they ducked together behind a massive twisted root.

A shout from behind them. "Sid! Go after them!" A string of curses. "I'll get the rifle."

David gripped Sandy's hand. A rifle! Where would he have to go to get that? Maybe the helicopter? Anyway, it would give them a few minutes.

"Come on," said Sandy, tugging at his arm. "We'll split up. He can only chase one of us at a time. We'll meet at *Kil-na-shee*."

"Right. You go that way. I'll go around."

She left the shelter of the root and started running. A shout. She thought she must have been seen. Sid would be coming after her. Then another shout.

"The boy! Get him!"

So much for equality, Sandy thought fleetingly.

They think the boy is more important. Well, she reassured herself, she had given David a few extra moments, at least. She risked a quick look around.

David was making for the standing forest. The tangled trunks were giving him trouble, but they were hindering Sid too. He had had to change direction, so he wasn't gaining on David.

She caught a glimpse of Walter Stewart too, running the other way. Maybe he was going for a rifle, she thought. She hoped David would be in the forest by the time he was ready to fire it.

She turned and ran up the hill, and soon she was over the crest, hidden from anyone's view. She wanted to find the entrance to the cave as soon as she could, so she was glad they had found a marker to go by. She spotted it — the beak overhanging the sumach. There was no sign of pursuit. She pushed into the bush, careful to disturb the branches as little as possible. Just inside she crouched and waited, listening.

For what seemed like ages there was nothing. No sound. Even the forest was silent, holding its breath. It would take some time, she knew. David was circling around. Once in the standing forest he would make better time. But so would Sid.

"Come on, Davie," she pleaded. Then she heard him — or someone — pounding across the hillside. She prayed it was David. She peeked out. Yes, it was, but he didn't stop.

"Keep down," he hissed as he dashed by. "He's in sight."

Silence. Then more hurried footsteps. Heavy breathing passing by. Another long wait.

What felt like hours later, when she'd said and repeated her silent prayers, David slipped quietly back to the opening. Suddenly he was there, parting the branches.

"I've lost him," he gasped. "For a few minutes anyway. Let's make sure he doesn't notice anything."

And they were together in the close confines of *Kil-na-shee*.

* * *

"We'd better come up with a plan," Sandy whispered. They stood together near the cave mouth, behind the waterfall curtain, regaining their breath and composure.

"For the moment I guess we wait." David sat down on the cold stone, his back against the wall. "At least until we have time to think things over. They'll never find us here. We could always wait until they give up on us and go away."

"But *will* they? They can't afford to let us get to the police. They know we're here somewhere. They've got the helicopter — *two* of them if the other one comes back. They must think we're hiding in the forest, and sooner or later we'll have to go out into the open. Then they'll have us. Right?"

He nodded. "You're right. We can't just wait and see what happens. We have to *make* something happen. If we're going to walk out of here, it looks like we have three choices. One, there's Lost Road. We'd have to get there first, and at least the first few kilometres were chewed up by the tornado." He shook his head. "No, we'd never make it that way. Then there's the rail bed. I don't know where it goes, but it must lead somewhere — some town — sooner or later. And it would be easy walking. But we'd have to be on constant lookout for a helicopter, ready to run for cover — and there might be places where there isn't any." He shifted position on the hard stone. "That leaves the forest. We could walk due south, towards Collinton. We should be able to hide from the 'copters in the forest. Of course, we don't know how far it goes, certainly not all the way to town. But once out of the trees we'd find farms or houses. With telephones. It would be a long, hard walk."

"So you think the forest is our best chance?"

"Except it's so easy to lose your sense of direction in a forest. And my compass is back there in the Cherokee."

"Oh." Sandy digested that information for a moment. "How about your parents? Will they start to worry? Maybe call the local police here?"

"Not likely. If they hear about the tornado they'll just know about the little town that was hit. No reason to think we were in its path." He looked up, listening. "Hear that?"

She stood up and helped him to his feet. "Yes, another helicopter. Let's see what's going on." They moved to the side where they could watch the proceedings. A chopper came into view, circled, and settled onto the shore like a dragonfly. "Where are the binoculars?" He handed them to her.

"It's the other ones again. Mr. Redfern and Bull. They're talking to Mr. Stewart."

There were five men there now, including the two pilots. They were looking around, pointing, making sweeping circles with their arms. She handed the glasses to David. "Mr. Stewart has a gun."

"They must be desperate." He focussed the binoculars. "How would they ever explain murder by gunshot? You can't blame that on a tornado."

"You can be sure it would be only as a last resort," said Sandy. "But they have to stop us somehow. If that's the only way . . ." She paused, and put her hand on David's arm. "We have to get that compass, don't we?"

He lowered the glasses and looked at her. "Yes."

One of the helicopters started up, and lifted into the air. A moment later the other followed, leaving Walter Stewart alone. The choppers began to fly in widening circles, sweeping over the area.

"What do you suppose they'll do if they haven't

found us by dark?" Sandy said.

"I don't know. They know this area better than we do. And they're well aware that we *don't* know it, so I don't suppose they're worried yet. They'll assume we can't have gone far, and that we won't be going anywhere in the dark."

"But we will, won't we? Back to the Cherokee?"

He nodded slowly. "It'll be dark again soon. No moon. We'll have to be really careful. And we'll have to go the long way around the lake, along the south shore, just to make sure we're not seen from the lodge. But we have to get that compass."

16

Night was coming in fast. Only a dim grey gleam marked the place where the sun had vanished, and stars were beginning to show overhead.

Gloom gathered early in *Kil-na-shee*. While they waited for the night to get darker, Sandy and David ate some trail mix, careful to conserve their supplies for the long walk out to civilization. They were sitting side by side, well back from the spray of the falls, when they heard both helicopters start up again.

"Don't tell me they're leaving!" David stood and grabbed the binoculars. "That doesn't make sense."

First one chopper lifted, then the other, their navigation lights blinking. They circled briefly, strange black shapes against the darkening sky, then flew away in different directions.

"That's odd," he continued, puzzled. "I didn't think they'd leave until we were accounted for."

"The men haven't *all* gone surely?"

"Oh no, I doubt that. I was too late to see who was on board and who stayed behind, but I'm sure they didn't all leave. We know that the two pilots have gone, at least. And we can be sure they'll be back at first light for another search. So that leaves three at the most behind. Only three instead of five to worry about when we go back for the compass."

"Maybe we should start out now," Sandy suggested, "before it gets totally dark."

"Yes, you're right. We don't have to worry about being seen until we're on the rail bed and beyond the cliffs. By the time we get there it will be as dark as it's going to be."

"Shall we take the flashlight? It's not much use to us if we can't use it in case were spotted."

David hesitated. "We probably *should* leave it behind. On the other hand, it's going to be awfully difficult finding our way back to our hidden entrance here without it."

"So we'll compromise," said Sandy. "Let's leave it at the point where we join the rail bed — somewhere we can pick it up on the way back."

"Good idea. You're a genius."

"I know." Sandy grinned. "I have these attacks occasionally. We should wear dark clothing, too."

"And cover our faces with black stuff, if we had any black stuff. You don't have any black make-up, do you?"

"I don't have *any* make-up. What you see is what you get."

"It's that Scottish weather, I suppose. I hope that if you come to this country to live some day, you won't lose that rosy colour in your cheeks." He laughed. "For the moment, though, I can barely *see* your face, it's so dark. Ready?"

"Ready."

"Then let's go."

Some stars were visible through the interlaced branches overhead, but their light failed to penetrate as Sandy and David pushed through the sumac and paused, listening. Silence. The trees stood absolutely still. Not even the indefinable night sounds of the forest had begun yet.

David turned on the flashlight, but despite its occasional help, unexpected roots tripped them up and unseen branches whipped at their legs and faces. After a few moments he paused so they could take their bearings, and frowned. It would be so easy to lose their way. They should have started out earlier, but there was no point in dwelling on that mistake. He stopped suddenly as the ground in front of his left foot vanished. "Holy smoke! What *is* this?" He grabbed Sandy's hand. "We must have — Oh, I know. It's the rail bed, where they had to cut through the rock. Somehow we've got way above it."

"Well, at least we've found it," said Sandy. "We'll have to backtrack and go around."

"Right."

A few minutes later they were on the level of the rail bed itself. It stretched away in both directions along the lake's southern shore, into impenetrable darkness. Even the stars were beginning to withdraw behind encroaching clouds.

"Good," whispered David. "The darker the better, now that we're here. We'll have easy going along here, until we get to the far end of the lake. We don't have to worry about being seen until then. Now, where can we leave the flashlight?"

"Here," Sandy suggested. She indicated a spot where the cut started and the resulting cliff began its ascent. "Right here, beside the track. We don't want to hide it, or we won't find it when we come back."

"Okay. Below this bush." David set it down at the base of a lone shrub. "Now, we're off."

They started out, hand in hand, into the silent night. There were weeds growing on the rail bed, but it was easier going than the forest. They could soon make out the faint glimmer of the lake to their right, through the intervening line of trees. On their left was the indistinct line where the treetops pushed up into the sky.

They had not gone far when Sandy pulled David to a stop. "Listen," she whispered. "Hear that?"

"What? Oh, yes, it's the stream. The one we have to cross over. I forgot about that. And those planks — I wish we had the flashlight for this."

"We wouldn't dare use it anyway. We're almost directly across from the lodge now I think, and maybe it could be seen from there. We'll just have to feel our way." They could make out the white water now, boiling down the hillside to plunge through the dark gap that opened up before them. The planks they would have to use to cross over the stream were almost invisible.

"It didn't seem so frightening when we came this way yesterday," said David, "so why does it look dangerous now?"

"Because we can't see the far side. We can only see one step at a time, and that's scary."

David tested a few planks. "This end seems okay. I presume the other end is too — since I'm sure no one else has been this way since yesterday. We'd better go one at a time, though, and me first. If the planks hold my weight, they'll hold yours. Wait till I give you the okay."

He put out one foot, balancing his weight between two planks, and edged forward. Then another foot. Another. The planks gave a little as he neared the centre of the bridge, and he could hear the hungry water seething far below, but he didn't dare stop. He went on, breath suspended, as the boards trembled. He could feel them almost bouncing with each step. He altered his gait to a shuffle, barely lifting his feet, until the vibrating stopped. The footing felt firmer now. He let his breath out in relief as he stepped onto the far bank.

"Okay, Sandy," he called softly. "The planks give a bit, but they'll hold. Just take your time."

"I'm coming." She was a black shadow in the darkness, creeping toward him. Then she was just a few steps away. He reached out his hand to welcome her to safety, but she brushed past it and put her arms around him instead. "Oh," she breathed. "That *was* scary."

"Sure was, but it's plain sailing now," he said, "at least until we're past the lake."

They went on, now more confident. They would have to go through more dense bush to round the western end of the lake, but they would tackle that problem when they reached it. Meanwhile there was no chance that they would be seen from across the lake either from the lodge or their former campsite, even though the line had been built up here, with ditches dropping away on either side. The thick wall of darkness would hide them, so long as they didn't use a light. With luck, they would make good time while the coast was clear and the walking easy.

David was beginning to feel the excitement of

success when, almost before he could grasp what it was, a danger signal flashed into his brain. He froze, then squinted into the darkness. A tiny red glow, somewhere ahead, that flared and vanished in an instant. A tiny red glow where no glow should have been.

17

"A cigarette!" David hissed. "Someone's there, smoking a cigarette!"

"Where? I didn't —"

He grabbed Sandy and was pulling her down into one of the ditches alongside the embankment, when he stumbled and fell, with her on top of him. They rolled down, down to where tall reeds grew on the shore of the lake.

"Davie!" Sandy gasped. "What on earth —"

"Someone there," he whispered. "Not far ahead. We almost walked right into him. He's smoking. I saw the glow."

"Are you sure? It wasn't a firefly, was it?"

"No. Shh. Don't move. I don't think he saw us, but in another moment he would have. Listen . . ." But there was nothing. Not a sound.

Sandy took a deep breath. "They're waiting there for us!" she whispered. "Why did they think we might be coming along here?"

David shifted his weight to let Sandy roll free. "Because they're smarter than I am. You saw how easy it was going along the line. We could have walked along there all night and got a long way by daylight. *I* never thought of that, but they did. I'll bet there are more of them waiting back there, in the other direction, too."

"So what do we do now? Circle back again?"

David shook his head. "Oh, if only I'd had time to think! We could have gone into the *other* ditch, not this one. If we can get back across the rail line, we could go around them in the forest. Do you think we could make it there without being seen?"

Sandy looked anxiously overhead. The clouds that had been gathering were in retreat. The stretch of glittering stars was expanding, their light reaching down to relieve a little of the darkness. "I don't think so. It would be risky."

"But we'll never get past them on this side. There isn't enough room between the rail line and the lake," David said.

"Maybe we could. The reeds are high. I wonder how deep the water is. Can you swim without making a racket, Davie?"

"Swim in there?" David said. "You've got to be kidding."

"No I'm not. I'm going to check the water. If it's deep enough . . ."

"Sandy! What are you doing?"

"Taking off my shoes. I'll tie them around my neck. Shh now. Here goes."

In a moment he had lost her among the reeds. Then he heard a muted splash, the movement of water, and before long she was back, pushing through the reeds, whispering. "It's about waist deep. That's deep enough. We can swim, close in to the shore."

He hesitated only a moment. "Okay." He took off his shoes, stuffed his socks into them and tied them around his neck, and followed her. His feet were in muck, then into water with a stony bottom. He shivered as the cold crept up his legs.

"Go easy," she whispered. "It drops away suddenly, but only to your waist. I'll go ahead." And she was gone.

He had a momentary vision of her slipping deeper into the water until she was swimming. He could see only her head, then he lost even that below the reeds. He pushed out to follow her, swimming silently in about a metre of water.

He paused, drifting, to take his bearings. How far ahead had that cigarette glow been? Probably not far, but he couldn't be sure. It was impossible to tell in the darkness. Better to err on the side of safety than to leave the water too soon. Where was

Sandy? He still couldn't see her. That was good. She was still going, so he would too . . .

Suddenly, a voice, not much more than a whisper, almost directly above him: "What was that?"

He caught his breath.

"What was what?"

Another voice. So there *were* two of them . . .

"I heard something. In the water."

A shaft of light shot out onto the lake. David had a quick glimpse of Sandy, just beyond the edge of the light beam. She was there, then she was gone. Expanding ripples marked her place.

"Put out that blasted light!" A hoarse, urgent whisper. "If those kids are anywhere near you'll give us away."

"But there's something there." Nevertheless the light was doused.

David froze. He crouched there in the water, only his head above the surface. He stared up into the darkness where the light had been.

"Something went into the water. You can see the ripples."

"So, it's a fish. Or an otter. For sure it's not those kids in that shallow ditch. That's all we have to worry about."

But the second man continued to peer into the water.

David could make him out now, a darker shadow in the night. He held his breath. He didn't dare move. The man would see him, if he looked that way. Maybe, if he remained perfectly still, he could be mistaken for a rock. He prayed that Sandy had surfaced again, somewhere farther on.

He took a deep breath as the second man stepped closer, into the reeds. For a moment he considered ducking under the surface. But only for a moment. He'd give himself away for sure if he tried that. His only hope was to stay still. Slowly, slowly, he turned so that the faint blur of his face would not be visible from the shore.

But now he couldn't see what was going on. There was a swishing noise, then something moving in the water. *He has a stick!* David realized, trying to sink down even farther. *He's beating the reeds, probing the shoreline. How long can I stay like this? How long before he realizes we're here?*

The stick moved close to his head, splashing water over him, moved on, came back, brushed across the top of his head. David almost cried out. He bit his lip hard, waiting for the shout of discovery. What could they do if they were seen? Could he and Sandy evade the men in the darkness? What if they were armed?

"Come on, don't be a fool," the first man muttered. "There's nothing there."

Listen to him, pleaded David soundlessly. *Listen to your friend. There's nothing here but fish and rocks.*

He heard a shuffling in the reeds. Was the man leaving? He didn't dare turn to look. Not yet. Don't give yourself away now. Just another few minutes.

The shuffling ceased. There was no further sound. Then he heard voices, two voices, coming from back along the rail bed. Thank God! The man had given up.

At last David moved. He took a deep breath, dove, and swam almost scraping along the bottom, pulling himself forward by grabbing at rocks, so he wouldn't have to move his feet. He forced himself to take it slowly, to keep going until his lungs were about to burst. Then he edged up above the surface. For a moment he could see nothing but the faint sheen of the water and the obscure sweep of reeds at the water's edge. Then an urgent whisper.

"Davie! Here." And there was Sandy, moving out of the shadows below the reeds, clutching him.

"We're well past them now," she whispered. "But we still have to be careful. We'd better keep to the ditch from now on. The helicopter is there, did you know?"

"What? Where?"

"Back there, where those men are. On the rail bed."

"Oh. So *that's* where they went."

They pulled themselves out of the water, shivering, their clothes clinging to their bodies, cold and clammy. The shoes they had hoped to keep dry were soaked. They squelched along in the ditch, while the lake gleamed pale on their right and the rail embankment loomed on the left, below the dark forest background. Overhead, the stars played hide and seek behind scattered clouds.

They would have to return this way. That disquieting thought was in the back of their minds. But first they had to retrieve the compass. One thing at a time . . .

The lake gave way, at last, to forest. It stood before them, black and daunting, between them and their objective. At least the tall trees here had limited the light that could filter through, so there was little undergrowth to fight. They walked on a springy carpet of pine needles and dead leaves that rustled underfoot, advancing from one black sentinel tree to the next. Finally they rounded the western edge of the lake, where the forest gave way, and they were out in the open once more.

Along the northern shore that led down to their old campsite was some of the worst aftermath of the tornado. They picked their way through and over the debris, up to the top of the hill. The valley was below them now, an opaque abyss relieved only by the faint sheen of the lake. The lodge was somewhere over there to the right, below the far hill.

They descended the hill cautiously. Soon they could make out the strange shape of the backhoe, and beyond that the hump of the Cherokee with its back end stuck out of the water. They stopped beneath one of the few trees that still stood unharmed.

"Okay," whispered David, "you keep watch. If you see anything — like a light over there in the direction of the lodge — you'll have to warn me. Can you whistle like a bird? Or hoot like an owl?"

"It better be an owl at this time of night. Don't worry. I'll warn you somehow."

"Okay. I won't be long. I know just where the compass is." He gave her hand a quick squeeze, then slipped away, moving like a shadow.

Sandy tried to follow his path in the darkness. He was in the water now, wading out to the car. He would only be a minute or two . . .

An arm wrapped around her waist. She started to scream but a hand clamped over her mouth. The scream died in her throat.

18

David waded out to the car, careful to move soundlessly. When he reached it he looked around quickly. Still no sign of life. Even Sandy was invisible, back there beneath the tree whose shape he could dimly make out. He unlocked the tailgate, lifting it just enough to reach in. But the compass wasn't there, not where he thought he had left it.

Blast! If only he had the flashlight. But no, he wouldn't dare use it anyway. He'd have to lean in, feel around. That meant letting the tailgate go up to its top position. He didn't want to do that. It would alter the shape of the Jeep's silhouette. But he had no choice.

He groped around on the floor. Where was it? He had left it right there in the corner, hadn't he? Well, it wasn't there now. Sandy had rummaged in here to fill the backpacks — she must have moved it. But it couldn't be far away. He moved his hand. What was that? Just the battered tent in its nylon bag. Nothing under it. The compass must be back even farther, maybe behind the driver's seat. He'd have to crawl right in.

He pulled the tailgate down behind him, careful not to close it all the way. The click of the catch would sound like a pistol shot on a night like this. He started to feel around under the seat, then stopped. Something was wrong. He didn't know what, but he was sure of it. It wasn't something he had seen — he couldn't see a blasted thing. Something he had heard, without realizing it? Maybe. All he knew was that something was wrong. There was danger nearby.

He raised his head to look out the back window. Nothing but that black void. He stared into it until his eyes ached, trying to make out more than that indistinct line where the spiky trees broke the skyline. Nothing. Was he just imagining something wrong? Where was Sandy? Over there somewhere, keeping watch. She was going to warn him if anything was wrong but she hadn't. So everything must be all right.

A shaft of light shot out of nowhere, swept across the beach, transfixing the Jeep in its glare. David ducked down. Had he been in time? He couldn't be sure. He was aware of the light moving above his head, probing the interior. Was it noticeable that the tailgate wasn't securely closed? No, surely not. What about Sandy? She must be frantic.

The light moved away. With deliberate care David raised his head. He watched anxiously, nerves on edge, as the light swept toward the tree where Sandy had been waiting. She wasn't there. He drew in a relieved breath. She had had time to hide, then . . . But the only place to hide was behind the tree, and it wasn't a very big one. The light lingered there, as if whoever was holding it was suspicious. But there was no sign of her.

David tried to piece it together. She *must* be there, behind the tree. If she didn't move, she wouldn't be seen. Whoever it was couldn't be sure they were here, could he?

The light was lowered. For a moment it dimly outlined the shape of the man who was holding it. He was also holding a walkie-talkie, and seemed to be speaking into it.

What was he saying? It's a false alarm? There's no one here? Or was he convinced of that? No, apparently not. David ducked lower. The man was approaching again, wading through the water, raising the light to the tailgate window.

The game was up. He couldn't hope to escape detection this time. There was only one chance.

He crouched against the tailgate, waiting. The light was coming closer. Then it was right above him, shining down onto him.

Now! He thrust his whole weight against the tailgate. It shot up. There was a crack, a cry of pain. A light arced through the air, hit the water, glowing there for a moment, then vanishing. He heard the body splash backward into the water as his own momentum carried him headlong, face down. He swallowed a mouthful of water. Then he was lurching up and running, running for the shore.

He didn't make it. Two more black shapes emerged to block his way.

19

Sandy stood pinned, unable to twist away from the grip of the arm around her. Her heart hammered against her ribs.

Then a craggy face brushed against her cheek and a voice spoke, barely a whisper, into her ear. "Shh. Don't move." Then, seconds later, "It's Dan. Remember me? I'm a friend. Now don't make a sound. There's a man on watch not ten metres away."

A friend! Panic, then relief, then bewilderment left Sandy trembling. A friend? Of course, Dan, the auxiliary constable . . . The arm still held her, but the hand moved away from her mouth.

The whisper came again. "What's David doing?"

"Going — " She turned her head to whisper to the man behind her. "Going for a compass. So we can go back. Through the forest."

"I hope he makes it." The hold on her slackened. "There's a man over there, by the water. If it's dark enough, he might be okay — Shoot!"

"What? What is it?"

"The tailgate's up."

She could see that now. The shape of the shadow that was the Jeep had altered, but only for a moment or two. Then the gate was down again. Unless the man near the water had been looking right in that direction he could have missed it.

Near the shoreline the beam from a flashlight split the darkness. A man, no more than a darker shade of night, was moving to the water's edge, casting the light onto the Jeep. It seemed to reveal nothing. The light started to move.

"Come on." Sandy was pulled back into the meagre protection of the tree. "Down. Don't move. Cover your face."

She flung herself as flat as possible, and turned her face away from the approaching circle of light. She was aware of it passing above her, taking forever. Then it was gone. The night was blacker than ever. Cautiously she raised her head.

The light was still on, aimed down at the ground. It showed the shadowed figure of a man speaking into a walkie-talkie. Sandy couldn't make out his words, but Dan caught something.

"He saw something. He's calling the helicopter.

We've got to get David — Shh."

The man with the flashlight was moving again, wading out into the water. He shone his light right into the back window of the Jeep.

"Come on!" Dan caught Sandy's arm, running.

They heard a crack, a sudden confusion of sound, saw moving shadows, the flashlight arcing through the air and vanishing. Then someone floundering in the water, lurching up, coming toward them, stopping short at sight of them.

"Davie!" Sandy cried. "It's all right. It's me. And Dan."

"What? Who . . . ?"

"Dan Ketchawa. But the man with the flashlight, what happened to him?"

"I . . . I don't know." David turned, expecting to see the man coming after him, but there was no sign of movement. "What the heck . . . ?"

"Come on." Dan took a flashlight from his pocket and shone it by the Jeep. The man was lying on his back, not moving, his face barely above water. It was George Redfern. The cut under his chin was dripping blood.

"He'll be all right," said Dan. "You gave him quite a whack with the tailgate and he's out like a light, but maybe not for long. We'd better get him onto dry land. If he rolls over he might drown."

Still in a daze, David grabbed one limp arm and helped Dan drag George Redfern onto the beach.

"Quick," Dan hissed. "We haven't much time. He was calling the 'copter, and it could be here any minute. It'll have landing lights if nothing else, and there may not be time to get back to the trees." He looked around. "We need to hide somewhere."

"The lodge!" David cried. "We could get around to the far side." He looked across the lake, to where the helicopter must be. No sign of anything yet.

"How about inside the lodge?" Dan countered. "Part of it's still standing."

"Walter Stewart might still be somewhere in there," Sandy warned. "At the back."

"Walter Stewart!" Dan slowed to a jog. "*He's* in on this?" He whistled. "That puts a different light on things. What the heck's going on here anyway?"

David came to a stop, breathing hard. "You mean you don't know? They're slaughtering animals, for gall bladders and livers and antlers — things like that."

"*What*? Walter Stewart and George Redfern are in on *that* ugly business? We should have let George drown back there. No, drowning's too good for him. But what makes you think Stewart might still be in there?"

"He *was* here, and unless he went away in one of the helicopters . . ."

"No, I saw them take off. Bull and the pilot in one helicopter, and just the pilot in the other. So Stewart's still here somewhere. Are you kids sure about this slaughter business?"

"Oh yes. There's a bear's carcass hanging up in there, and a pile of antlers, and a freezer filled with packages. All clearly labelled."

"Plus a pair of bear cubs," Sandy added, "except we let them out of their cage and they made it into the woods."

"I'd say it's a big operation," David continued. "There's a radio transmitter in there too. That's how they communicate with the outside world."

"Okay." Dan's voice was grim. "We can forget about just getting away from here. My radio's in my car, and I had to leave it way back along Lost Road. *And* I smashed my hand-set when I fell over one of those blasted trees. By the time we can get help they could have removed some of their stuff by 'copter. Enough to implicate them as the poachers, at least. Then it would be your word against Walter Stewart's. And he's a big man in these parts."

"So what can we do?" David asked

"We'll have to use their transmitter. I'll call Jeff Wilks."

"As soon as Mr. Stewart hears the helicopter start up, he's bound to come out to see what's going on," Sandy warned. "And I expect he'll come out through the tower, where the transmitter is. That means we should go in through the basement."

"You're right," David said. "Let's go. We can use

your flashlight if we're careful. It's an obstacle course in there, and if we trip on something and Stewart hears us, we'll just give ourselves away."

Dan handed his flashlight to David. "Lead the way."

They clambered through the debris that had been the lodge. Occasional use of the flashlight led them over the worst parts, and past the counter they had sheltered under. They had reached the adjoining room when David extinguished the flashlight. The *chop-chop* of the approaching helicopter was getting louder. Then it swept overhead, its landing light dazzling. In a moment it would settle onto the beach in front of the lodge.

"Quiet," David whispered. "That should bring Stewart on the run."

He was right. A light appeared outside. A man ran by, not glancing in their direction.

"Right. Come on." He led the way down through the basement, through the cupboard, and into the hallway. His light shone through the door that he and Sandy had smashed in their escape.

Dan followed them in. "Look at all this gear. This must have been going on for a long time."

David pointed to the inner door. "Take a look in there."

One glance was all Dan needed. He shuddered. "Okay." He turned to the transmitter. "You two keep watch. I'll contact the OPP. I don't suppose there are any firearms down here? There must be rifles if they're shooting the animals."

"Mr. Stewart had one," Sandy said. "I think he got it out of the helicopter. I haven't seen any others."

"Then we'll have to do without. Let me know if they come this way. I hope the police have a chopper handy."

Sandy and David went out and up the stairs leading into the tower, feeling their way over the rubble until they were outside. They crept alongside the wall until they could see around the corner of the lodge. One helicopter was on the beach, its landing light beaming out in a great yellow circle around it, casting weird shadows. Several men stood grouped around the body on the ground.

As Sandy and David watched they saw George Redfern stagger up to a standing position. After a moment the others began to spread out, lights swinging in all directions. The chopper's engine broke into life and it lifted, the circle of light beneath it widening.

"We'd better go," whispered David. "If that 'copter flies above us they'll see us. Uh-oh!" He ducked down.

The other helicopter was coming. It appeared over the hill behind the lodge, illuminating the battered path of the tornado, throwing everything into stark relief as it approached the place where

Sandy and David crouched beside the lodge. There was no escaping its all-revealing glare.

In seconds it swept over them, blinding them, then plunging them back into total darkness. But the damage was done.

A voice shouted in triumph. The helicopter came around again, the wind from its blades beating down on them. They were in the spotlight, centre stage, with nowhere to go.

Walter Stewart stepped into the circle of light, a rifle under his arm. "Well well," he said. "You two have given us a merry chase. But we're not going to give you any more leeway, I assure you." He motioned with the gun. "Come this way."

David took a slight step forward. "This way" was toward the beach. Good. That would give Dan a little more time on the transmitter before they found out what Mr. Stewart had in mind.

"We've got them." The man spoke into a hand mike. "Come on down. I've got a job for one of you."

Sandy's hand crept into David's.

Bull came forward, showing the way with a powerful light, directing them around to the front of the lodge, along the overgrown walk to the beach, while the helicopters settled, their rotors slowing.

"Now," said Stewart, "you're going for a ride. Even been in a chopper before?"

David knew, then, what he had in mind. Bodies dropped from a great height could easily be mistaken for bodies battered to death by a tornado. "No," he said. "And we're not going now either."

"I think you are, one way or another. Bull, tie their hands — "

"*I wouldn't do that.*" The voice came out of the darkness, startling in its calmness.

"What the blazes!" Stewart spun around, the rifle coming up.

Bull turned his light in the direction of the voice. "Dan Ketchawa!"

Dan stood there, unarmed, his hands at his sides. "You're in enough trouble now, all of you, without adding murder to your crimes. I've just been talking to the police in Collinton. They'll be here in a few minutes. You've had it."

"I don't think so, Dan," Stewart said, grinning. "*I've* got the gun, haven't I?"

"But *we* pulled the plug, Mr. Stewart." David tried to keep his voice calm, and his face impassive. "When we found out what you were doing, we figured we could at least wreck your chance of profiting from it. All those little packages you had in the freezer are half-thawed by now."

"You *what!*" Stewart whirled to the side. "Bull, go check — "

In that one moment Dan leapt forward, knocked the rifle out of Stewart's hands, and scooped it up from the ground. "As I said, Stewart, you've had it."

20

"So that stuff they said about ghosts and hauntings — none of that was for real?" David said.

Dan spooned sugar into his coffee. "Not a word of it. It was all for your benefit, to put you off going to Lost Lake."

They were sitting in the police station, so late that it was nearly morning, thinking back to the last conversation they'd had in the Pagoda.

"Mr. Stewart, George Redfern, and Bull were all in the Pagoda. Was that by accident?" David added.

"I doubt it. I expect Walter Stewart arranged it."

"What about Mr. Beakham? Was he in on it too?" Sandy asked.

"The Beak? No, doesn't look like it. A little imagination can turn any derelict building into a haunted house. The kids around here did make up stories about it and dared each other to go there, but no one ever did. They had no way to get there, so it was safe to tell tall tales about it. You notice they didn't object too much when they found out you were only staying overnight, and not likely to explore the lodge."

"But one of them said there were native legends about Lost Lake Lodge being haunted," David said. "Is that part of it true?"

Dan laughed. "They must have got a shock when I spoke up — they didn't know I was there — and even more of a shock when I went along with them. As far as I know there never have been any native legends connected with the lodge. It was built way after any native people lived near the lake. And I should know. I'm one of them."

"So why did you play along with them?"

"Because it looked like they didn't want you to go to the lake, and I didn't mind that idea. I figured someone might be using the lodge as a base for small-time poaching, taking the odd moose out of season. I never dreamed they were into it on such a big scale. Anyway, I thought it would be best if you stayed away until I had a chance to find out what was going on."

"What tipped you off enough to come all the way up there, then?"

"I went in to Bill Blake's garage the next morning to find out if you had left. He said you had. He also told me he thought someone might have tried to tamper with your brakes."

"What? He didn't tell me that when I picked the Jeep up."

"He wasn't really sure himself, though he couldn't see how he'd missed something like that. I knew then that you might be in real danger. But before I could do anything, the tornado went through and I got called to go up to Burns Falls. I came as soon as I was able to get away from there, and took the car in as far as I could — about ten klicks from the lodge — then walked in the rest of the way. I arrived about dusk, in time to see the two helicopters take off, and one of them land just over on the other side of the lake. I couldn't figure *that* out. There was no sign of you two, of course. I had no idea what had happened to you.

"I decided to hang around for a while, all night if necessary, to see what was going on. Then a man came and took up a position over by the beach. Looked like he was set to stay awhile. A little while later you two came out of the woods. I knew I had to warn you about the man on watch, but obviously I couldn't call out. So I had to go after you."

"We had no idea you were there," David said.

"My people are supposed to be able to glide through the forest without so much as snapping a twig, aren't we?" Dan grinned. "But seriously, by the time I caught up with you I was too late to stop

David from leaving the trees. And I guess I scared the living daylights out of you, Sandy. Sorry about that."

"You did," agreed Sandy. "But you saved our necks, so I'll forgive you. I'm just glad the police showed up when they did, too."

Dan nodded. "They had trouble rounding up a chopper on short notice, so it's just as well David surprised Walter Stewart the way he did. That 'pulling the plug' lie was quick thinking."

"I'm just glad it worked," David said. "Do you think we'll have to testify?"

"Possibly, but not necessarily. The evidence is all there. No way Stewart and his men can get out of this one. No, you can go home and forget about Lost Lake for awhile."

"Not for long. We'll be back for the Cherokee. We'll have to see if Bill Blake can tow it out and fix it up for us, then we'll drive back in again. There's still canoeing time left this fall, and I think I've talked Sandy into staying awhile longer. *This* time there'll be nothing to spoil our fun."

"Besides," said Sandy, "there are certain matters we have to discuss — " her foot nudged David's under the table " — and only one appropriate place to discuss them."

Dan looked from one to the other. "Where's that?"

"A place," said David, "called *Kil-na-shee*."

Robert Sutherland grew up in Ontario, but his British parents introduced him to English adventure stories and magazines like *Boys' Own* and *Chums Annual*. During the Second World War he served in the Royal Canadian Navy for three years, a stint that reinforced his love for the sea. His books often feature a sea or lake setting, whether it's the windswept Hebrides of Scotland in *Mystery at Black Rock Island*, *The Ghost of Ramshaw Castle*, and *Death Island*, or the mysterious lakes of northern Ontario in *The Loon Lake Murders* and *If Two Are Dead*.